PUFFIN

ENIGMA

ERIC WALTERS is one of Canada's best-known and most prolific writers of fiction for children and young adults. He has published more than eighty novels with more scheduled for the coming years. His books have won over 100 awards, including eleven separate children's choice awards, and have been translated into thirteen languages around the world. He is the only three-time winner of both the Ontario Library Association Silver Birch and Red Maple Awards.

Also by Eric Walters from Penguin Canada

The Camp X Series

Camp X
Camp X: Camp 30
Camp X: Fool's Gold
Camp X: Shell Shocked
Camp X: Trouble in Paradise
Camp X: Enigma

The Rule of Three
Shattered
The Bully Boys
Just Deserts
Fly Boy
Wounded
Black and White
Voyageur
The Falls
The Pole
Sketches
Elixir
Run
Royal Ransom
Trapped in Ice
The Hydrofoil Mystery

ERIC WALTERS

CAMP

X

ENIGMA

PUFFIN

an imprint of Penguin Canada Books Inc., a Penguin Random House Company

Published by the Penguin Group
Penguin Canada Books Inc., 90 Eglinton Avenue East, Suite 700, Toronto, Ontario, Canada M4P 2Y3

Penguin Group (USA) LLC, 375 Hudson Street, New York, New York 10014, U.S.A.
Penguin Books Ltd, 80 Strand, London WC2R 0RL, England
Penguin Ireland, 25 St Stephen's Green, Dublin 2, Ireland (a division of Penguin Books Ltd)
Penguin Group (Australia), 707 Collins Street, Melbourne, Victoria 3008, Australia
(a division of Pearson Australia Group Pty Ltd)
Penguin Books India Pvt Ltd, 11 Community Centre, Panchsheel Park, New Delhi – 110 017, India
Penguin Group (NZ), 67 Apollo Drive, Rosedale, Auckland 0632, New Zealand
(a division of Pearson New Zealand Ltd)
Penguin Books (South Africa) (Pty) Ltd, 24 Sturdee Avenue, Rosebank, Johannesburg 2196, South Africa

Penguin Books Ltd, Registered Offices: 80 Strand, London WC2R 0RL, England

First published in Puffin paperback by Penguin Canada Books Inc., 2013

Published in this edition, 2014

1 2 3 4 5 6 7 8 9 10 (WEB)

Copyright © Eric Walters, 2013

*Publisher's note: This book is a work of fiction. Names, characters, places, and incidents either are the product of the author's
imagination or are used fictitiously, and any resemblance to actual persons living or dead, events, or locales is entirely
coincidental.*

Manufactured in Canada.

LIBRARY AND ARCHIVES CANADA CATALOGUING IN PUBLICATION

Walters, Eric, 1957–, author
   Enigma / Eric Walters.

(Camp X)
Originally published: Toronto, Ontario, Canada : Puffin, 2013.
ISBN 978-0-14-318711-0 (pbk)

1. World War, 1939–1945—Secret Service—Juvenile fiction. I. Title.
II. Series: Walters, Eric, 1957– . Camp X.

PS8595.A598E65 2014   jC813'.54   C2014-904170-5

eBook ISBN 978-0-14-319039-4

Visit the Penguin Canada website at **www.penguin.ca**

Special and corporate bulk purchase rates available; please see
www.penguin.ca/corporatesales or call 1-800-810-3104.

For William Stephenson—a great Canadian hero

CHAPTER ONE

THE SHIP ROLLED in one direction and my stomach lurched in another. I felt sick, but I was pretty sure I wasn't going to throw up again because there was basically nothing left in my stomach. Supper had long since abandoned ship.

I opened my eyes. It was so dark I couldn't even see the ceiling of the little cabin we were sleeping in, but I knew it was only a couple of feet above my bunk. Even the cabin's porthole was covered with a blackout screen. It was almost as if my eyes were still closed. There was nothing wrong with my hearing, though—in the bunk below me my brother Jack was snoring. It sounded more

1

like somebody sawing wood. Funny, though, I sort of liked the noise. It let me know I wasn't alone. It was a little bit of reassurance in the middle of a very big ocean.

The ship pitched violently and I had to brace myself so I wouldn't be tossed out of the bunk and onto the floor. This wasn't working. I wasn't going to sleep. I felt like I was suffocating, unable to draw air into my lungs, trapped in this pitch-black, stuffy, stifling hot and heaving cabin. Maybe some fresh air would help.

Holding on with both hands to the bed rail, I sat up and then spun around, feeling for the ladder with my feet. Slowly, rung by rung, I climbed down.

"What are you doing?" Jack asked sleepily.

"I'm going on deck for a breath of air."

"Go to sleep."

"I can't. Too sick. I think I might throw up again."

"You are such a landlubber," Jack said.

"And who are you, Popeye the Sailorman?"

"*I yam what I yam and that's all what I yam*," he said. Jack was older than me—all of fifteen—but he still loved a good Popeye cartoon. "How long is it going to take for you to get your sea legs, anyway?"

"Maybe longer than we have. I just want to get my feet on solid ground."

Jack had been just a little nauseated for the first day or so, and our mother and father had hardly seemed bothered at all. But me? Three days at sea and I *still* hadn't adjusted.

The ship heaved violently to one side and I had to grab the edge of the bunk to keep from tumbling over. I had the sensation that the whole ship was dropping down while my guts were lurching in the opposite direction.

"I gotta go!" I exclaimed. I reached out blindly to where I thought the door was and fumbled around until I found the handle.

"Don't do anything stupid!" Jack yelled as I yanked open the door.

"I'm just going up top to get some air."

"Then don't fall overboard!"

"I'll try not to."

"Good, because we won't waste any time going back to try and find you," Jack said.

"Nice to know you care."

I stumbled into the narrow corridor and closed our

cabin door behind me. There wasn't much light—one small lamp up the way—but it was more than enough to see by. Slowly, with a hand on the railing on either side, I bumped along the passage, passing my parents' room and those occupied by officers. The enlisted men—the ship was transporting almost a thousand of them—were all in much bigger rooms on the lower decks. Sleeping in bunk beds stacked three high, they were like sardines crammed into a can.

Stumbling along with each lurch of the ship, I came to the door to the stairs. It was sealed shut with a waterproof hatch, and I struggled to lower the big handle and disengage the teeth locking it in place. I stepped through the opening and closed the door behind me. Careful to keep a firm grip on the railings, I started up the steps, the sound of my feet echoing up and down the stairwell. We were only two flights below the deck, and as I climbed, the clean smell of the sea air became stronger.

I stopped at the top, my progress blocked by a second metal door. There was a little porthole where normally I could have seen out, but the glass had been covered over with black paint so no light would ever escape out into the night. I pushed down on the handle and opened it up. Stepping out, I was slapped in the face by a shower of ocean spray, which shocked me fully awake. I thought about going back inside, but the cold air and ocean water were probably the jolt I needed to get over my queasiness.

I slammed the big metal hatch behind me and it closed with a heavy thud.

Standing beneath an overhang, still gripping the handle on the hatch, I looked past the railing and out to the ocean. Waves towered like a giant wall of water and then fell away, allowing an occasional glimpse of sky and stars and moon. The deck was glistening, wet from the spray, pitching back and forth with the motion of the ocean. I was grateful I had gone to sleep in my clothes and shoes—the better to abandon ship if need be—but I remembered Jack's "joke" about being thrown overboard, and suddenly had doubts about being out there.

Then, as my eyes adjusted to the limited light, I realized I wasn't alone. Even though it was the middle of the night, four or five figures were hanging over the railing, holding on for dear life. Well, at least if a wave swept over the railing and tossed me into the ocean someone would be there to see . . .

I took a half-dozen quick steps on unsteady feet across the slick, rocking deck and grabbed the railing with both hands. Closer to the side and free of the overhang, the spray was much stronger. It felt good. The wet and the cool made my stomach feel better.

Close by on my left a seasick soldier hung over the railing, but he didn't seem to notice me. Even in the dim light I could see that he looked green. I turned in the other direction and saw more soldiers, heads hanging over the railing, equally oblivious. If they felt as bad as I did, I could understand why.

I heard a sound behind me and saw the hatch start to open. Maybe it was Jack coming up to see if I was—no, it was another soldier. He practically ran the distance from the door to the railing, almost bumped into me and immediately vomited over the side into the ocean. I sidled away, trying to get some distance between us for the sake of my own delicate stomach.

He looked over. "Sorry about that."

"I think I understand." And as if to prove it, I hurled up the remaining contents of my stomach.

"Feel a bit better now?" he asked.

"A bit. How about you?" I asked.

"I'll feel better when I'm ashore." He paused, and for a second I thought he was going to heave again, but he didn't. "Funny, when I decided to enlist I was having a hard time deciding if I should join the army or the navy. I flipped a coin. Lucky for me it landed tails or I'd be a sailor now."

"I'm sure you'd get used to it . . . eventually."

"I hope I never have to find out," he said. "At least it's getting less rough."

I hadn't really thought about it, but looking out, I realized he was right. The ship was still rising up and down but the waves were lower, the sea flatter than it had been since we'd set sail.

"I've seen you around," the soldier said. "I thought it was strange that there was a family on board with all these troops."

"My mother would agree with you," I said, although

I knew it was probably for different reasons. She didn't like us being around the soldiers because they were a "bad influence." There certainly was a lot of drinking going on, and it was hard to turn down a corridor without bumping into a game of dice or cards. I'd also heard more than a few words that I'd heard before but would never have said out loud with such gusto and frequency.

"So, is your family important?" the soldier asked.

"Not particularly. We're just going home to England, where my father has been stationed."

"Home?"

"Yeah, we're English," I lied.

"Really? Maybe my ears are working as badly as my stomach, but I'd have sworn that was a Canadian accent you have."

"I was born in England, but we've been living in Canada so long I guess my accent has changed."

That was our cover story to explain why we were going to England. It was a lot more believable than the real story. While my father was stationed in Bermuda and Jack and I were at school there, my brother and I had met a real English princess, and we'd saved her from being kidnapped by Nazi agents. That was a few months back, but now that school was finally over for the year, we could accept the invitation we'd received from the royal family to come and visit. Apparently, they wanted to thank us . . . in person!

"Well, you sound just like a Canuck," the soldier said.

"So do you. Where are you from?" I asked. Better to get him answering questions instead of asking them.

"Me, I'm from Saskatoon, Saskatchewan."

"That doesn't even sound like a real place," I said. Although I knew where it was, I figured it was better to sound ignorant about Canada.

He huffed. "Just because you haven't heard of it doesn't mean it's not real. You bloody Brits are no better than the Yanks that way."

"Sorry, I didn't mean to offend you," I said, happy to know I could pass for a "bloody Brit."

"You should be sorry *and* grateful. We're crossing the pond to pull your biscuits out of the fire!"

"We are grateful, believe me," I said, trying my best to put on a bit of an English accent.

"I should apologize too. Not your fault. I guess I'm just not feeling very well . . . but you'd know all about that."

I nodded. We stood there side by side, holding the railing, trying not to allow the tossing of the ship to topple us over.

"It's good to have company," I said.

"Yeah, being out here alone would be dangerous," he said. "And speaking of company, she looks about the same size as us."

"*She? She* who?"

He laughed. "That ship, off our port side," he said, gesturing out over the ocean.

"Oh, yeah, of course."

A large ship was visible on the horizon. It was running dark, the same way we were, but its outline stood out against the sky, ever so slightly illuminated by the stars and moon. Beyond that, rising up on a wave, was a second ship, and I could just make out the dark shape of another beyond that.

"How many ships do you think there are in this convoy?" he asked.

"A lot, I guess."

"Me and the boys were trying to find out but the sailors are pretty tight-lipped about it . . . assuming they even know. We figure there have to be at least thirty."

"That's probably about right," I said. Actually, there were exactly forty-four cargo ships in the convoy. My father had told us. "Safety in numbers, I guess."

"I'm not so sure. Bigger convoys make a more attractive target for the U-boats," he said.

"I hadn't thought of that."

"There are *hundreds* of German submarines out there, you know. Not that I'm trying to scare you," he added hastily. "It's a big ocean and they're probably nowhere around us. Matter of fact, we have three destroyers escorting our convoy."

"That's good to know."

What was even better to know was that we actually had four destroyers, two corvettes, a mine-sweeper and a pocket cruiser in our escort group. I was only a twelve-year-old—well, closer to thirteen—but I was already used to having information that other people didn't have, just as I was used to not giving any information away. "Loose Lips Sink Ships" was the motto plastered on walls and trumpeted in the newsreels. Telling people information about ship movement could tip off the enemy wolf packs. It was a fact that at each port in North America there were spies watching the convoys forming and then trying to send that information to the U-boats waiting to intercept them. Out there, somewhere under the ocean, were hundreds of German submarines waiting to prey on the cargo ships.

"At least we're on the inside of the convoy, so we're protected by the other ships," I said.

"Not necessarily," the soldier said. "I heard that sometimes the U-boats come up inside the convoy, between the ships."

"But why would they do that?"

"The escorts, the destroyers, are all on the outside of the convoy. If a U-boat comes up inside it's harder for the destroyers to see, and even if they do see it, they can't really shell it. Then, after attacking, the U-boat can get lost underneath the cargo ships and disappear into the ocean."

"I guess that does make sense."

These convoys were part of the battle for the Atlantic

Ocean. Everything needed for the war effort—all the food and supplies and oil and weapons needed to fight, and for the civilians of England to survive—had to come across the ocean. Standing in the convoys' way were the wolf packs—groups of German submarines that were trying to sink the ships. Everybody had heard tales about ships being torpedoed, sunk, sent to the bottom, their crew and passengers lost beneath the waves of the cold North Atlantic.

"You know, all the ships, even the cargo ships, have men on watch for torpedoes and periscopes," the soldier said.

"I guess that's something." Not much—but something. I scanned the surface of the ocean, looking for periscopes. But a periscope was small and the ocean was big and the waves were so high you could practically hide a whole ship in the troughs. What chance did I have of seeing anything, and just what would I do if I *did* spot something?

"I'm feeling a bit better," the soldier said. "I think I'm going to head back inside."

"Me too. I guess I'll try to get some sleep."

I took one more look out at the ocean and then turned and headed for the hatch. The soldier had opened it up and was holding it for me. It would be good to get inside, and I could even change into some dry clothing.

"Thanks for—"

There was a loud blast. I spun around and the sky was on fire!

CHAPTER TWO

THE SHIP TO OUR port side had flames shooting out of the deck and into the sky!

The soldier and I stumbled back to the railing as the fire quickly spread, bathing the entire ship in light. Small figures, illuminated by the flames, scrambled along its deck.

The siren on our ship came to life, wailing away, and almost instantly the hatch opened and dozens of sailors came running out. Seconds later the searchlights on our ship, and on the ships around us, were criss-crossing the waves, searching for a U-boat! I couldn't help but think how my mother was going to react to all of . . . wait . . .

how was she going to react when she found I wasn't in my cabin?

I ran for the open hatch and fought my way through the soldiers who were streaming out onto the deck. I felt like a fish swimming upstream, and the current of soldiers just pushed me farther back onto the deck.

"Here, take this," a sailor said, handing me a life jacket.

"But it wasn't us that was torpedoed."

"This isn't over until—"

There was a massive explosion on the burning ship and I spun around to see flames shooting hundreds and hundreds of feet into the sky, throwing off so much light that the whole sky was as bright as day!

"It must have been carrying ammunition," the sailor yelled over the commotion as he ran off.

It seemed as if every inch of our deck was now filled. Soldiers from below had flooded up, and the sailors were at their stations—the searchlights and gun mounts were all manned, and the covers were being taken off the lifeboats. There couldn't possibly be enough lifeboats to carry all the soldiers on board. I decided putting on that life jacket wasn't such a bad idea.

Where were my brother and my mother and my father? My parents would have gone to our cabin and found Jack—and not me. They were going to be worried and angry, and they'd be getting angrier and angrier until they found me. I had to try to get back to our cabin.

There was another explosion from the torpedoed ship. It was listing badly to one side, the deck tilted so much that the railing on the near side was riding just above the waves. Flames fanned out over the whole vessel now. There was no question, it was going down. Men were jumping over the railing, abandoning ship. Already waiting for them were motor launches that had been sent out from our ship and others. Sailors were scooping up the men bobbing in the frigid water. I was terrified just thinking about it.

"Look over there!" somebody yelled, pointing.

I turned with everybody else to see a ship—a destroyer—cutting through the waves, moving in the direction of the rest of the ships. Its lights were blazing and it was moving so fast it was almost flying as its sleek silhouette cut between the cargo ships, its superstructure rising into the sky. A cheer went up from the crowd that was loud enough to drown out the wailing siren.

"Go get 'em, boys!" somebody yelled, and the crowd roared again. It reminded me of fans cheering at a hockey game.

The destroyer slipped right by, between us and the ship that had been hit, dodging past the motor launches picking up the survivors. It was so close to us that I could see sailors running on the destroyer's deck, men manning the guns. The cheering on our ship got louder and a couple of sailors on the destroyer waved at us as they went by. As soon as it passed, it turned hard to the starboard side so that it almost disappeared behind us.

Many of the soldiers scrambled to the other end of our deck, trying to keep the destroyer in sight, and I was pushed along by the crowd. As we watched, depth charges were launched from the destroyer—dozens of large barrels filled with explosives that shot up into the air and then plunged beneath the surface. Each barrel was armed with a device that would cause it to explode when it reached a certain depth—a depth they hoped would be close to the U-boat.

Anxiously I watched the spot where the charges disappeared, waiting for what would happen next . . . but

there was nothing . . . weren't they going to go off? Then
at last there was a loud *whoosh* and a funnel of water shot
up into the sky, followed immediately by a roar from the
soldiers all around me! What were they cheering for? Just
because it went off didn't mean that it had hit anything.

Suddenly a second, smaller warship appeared. It was
one of the corvettes, and it was moving even faster than
the destroyer. It seemed to be skimming over the crests
of the waves, not even dropping into the troughs between
them. Quickly it was closing in on our position, moving so fast and getting so close that for an instant I wondered if it was going to ram us. It made a turn and then
launched depth charges off its stern deck. They arced up
and then disappeared into the darkness right behind our
ship . . . did that mean the submarine was right underneath us?

In the ship's wake the surface of the water exploded,
sending a thunderous wave up so high and so close that
the sound of it was nearly deafening!

The destroyer had come about and was now steaming
up behind us. That U-boat had to be close for them to
keep making passes right by us and—a long, dark shape

burst through the surface! The explosion of the depth charges must have been strong enough and close enough to force the U-boat to rise. It practically leaped out of the water, right beside us!

The machine gun on our stern started firing—I could see the bullets hitting the hull of the U-boat. Then the deck hatch on the submarine opened and men began to stream out. Others started to drop out of the conning tower, bouncing off the deck and rolling into the water. They were so close I could almost see the expression on the face of each German sailor as he scrambled away. Some made it into the water and others were cut down by the machine-gun fire. Why were our guns still firing? The Germans weren't attacking, they were just trying to get away from the sinking ship!

The corvette had come back around, steaming forward, slicing through the water, headed right toward both the U-boat and the German sailors bobbing in the waves. Our machine guns went silent as the corvette made its pass between us and the U-boat. The water was littered with sailors struggling, swimming, and others who were simply floating—dead or injured. There were four motor launches skipping across the waves and they were picking up survivors. One of the launches went right up to the U-boat, now just barely above the water, and some of the Marines jumped onto its tilted deck. What were they—?

I was grabbed and practically yanked off my feet. "You idiot!" Jack yelled as he spun me around. "Do you know how worried Mom is?"

"I tried to get back!" I protested.

"Yeah, I can see how hard you're trying."

"I just sort of got shoved in this direction, and then the U-boat came up to the surface and—"

"There's a U-boat?"

"Right there, they got it."

Jack let go of my arm and pushed past me toward the railing.

"Wow, that's unbelievable," he said. "I never thought I'd see one of those again."

"Me neither."

Back at home, Jack and I had been standing right on the shore of the St. Lawrence River when another U-boat had been blown out of the water. It had been sent to pick up an important Nazi captain, an escapee from a prisonerof-war camp, and bring him back to Germany . . . and us with him! How strange to even think about that. It seemed more like a story I'd read than something that had actually happened to me.

"What are those Marines doing?" a man asked loudly.

"It looks like they're going into the U-boat," another exclaimed.

I tried to see through the darkness and the spray. The U-boat was falling into the distance as we kept steaming away, but I followed the path of those Marines along the deck, up the conning tower and then into the sub!

"Why would they go inside?" Jack asked.

"Maybe they're trying to capture the captain," I said. "He might still be in there, you know, going down with the sinking ship."

"Let him sink, let him drown!" a soldier who had overheard called out.

"Yeah, he would have drowned all of us if he could've," another said.

I understood how they felt, but I also knew that this had nothing to do with saving an enemy; it was all about interrogating him, getting important information.

A roar went up from the crowd and everybody, all at once, turned to face a different direction. I spun my head around. The torpedoed ship was slipping under the surface. The front deck and railing were already submerged and the tail section was rising up, higher and higher. There were a few men still on board and they slid helplessly down the deck, trying desperately to grab on to something before they were tossed into the sea.

As the side slipped under, there was a tremendous hiss as the sea water put out the flames and air escaped from the sinking vessel. Higher and higher the stern rose as more and more of the ship disappeared, slipping underneath the surface, faster and faster. And then it was gone. Nothing but silence. Not just from that ship, but from our ship as well. It was as if every single person was holding his breath. Even the wind dropped and the air was still, as if nature itself was taking a moment to honour the death of the vessel . . . the death of the men who went down with it.

"We have to go," Jack said. "Mom is going to be so angry with you. And worse than that, she's mad at me."

"Why at you?"

"She already yelled at me for letting you go above deck by yourself."

"I'll tell her you were asleep and didn't know," I said.

"I already told her I saw you go, but thanks for trying." He paused. "You know, you're not such a bad guy . . . for a little brother."

CHAPTER THREE

"QUIT SQUIRMING!" my mother ordered as she rubbed my hair with a towel.

I tried to stay still, but I was pretty sure that she was rubbing a whole lot harder than she needed to if she was only trying to dry my hair. There was at least a little bit of punishment involved in this.

"Really, sometimes you just don't think!" she said. "You have to learn to use your head for something other than holding your hat!"

Jack chuckled and she silenced him with a glare.

"I don't think you should be finding any of this

amusing," she snapped. "You're both lucky you're too big for me to put across my lap for a good spanking."

"Now, dear," my father said. "They're both all right."

"All right only if they don't catch their death from pneumonia! They're both soaked to the bone and freezing—as are you." My father had gone up on deck to search for me as well, and he was as soaked as Jack.

"It's not that cold," I said, although my chattering teeth told another story.

"They'll be fine," my father said. "Boys will be boys."

"It's not like I wanted to go up on deck," I said. "It was just that I was so seasick, and then when the ship was torpedoed and the U-boat was captured and the ship finally sank, it was really hard to leave."

"I don't think I could have left," my father admitted.

My mother didn't look too happy with him for saying that.

"We need to know where you are at all times," she insisted. "What if *our* ship had been torpedoed?"

"Well, I guess I would have been on deck already, ready to abandon ship," I said.

"He has a point," Jack added.

"What did I do to deserve living in a household with three men?" she exclaimed. "Why couldn't I have had at least one daughter?"

"Well," Jack said, "George isn't much of a boy, so you kinda got your wish."

"Shut up, Jack."

"No, you shut up!"

"Another fine example of exactly what I was saying," she said. "My sisters and I never talked to each other like that, ever. We cared for each other."

"They care for each other," my father said. "It's just that boys have a different way of showing love and affection."

"Insulting and punching each other is a way of showing love and affection? I'd hate to see what they'd do if they didn't like each other!"

"You'll never have to worry about that," my father said. "Now, boys, I want you both to apologize to your mother for making her worry and give her a big—"

There was a pounding on the cabin door.

"Who would be calling at this time of night?" my father asked.

I didn't know, but it gave me an uneasy feeling. I could

see from Jack's expression that he was feeling nervous as well. Anxiously I looked around the cabin, trying to locate my father's service revolver. His holster was empty, and it wasn't any place I could see, so it had to be in one of the drawers, or in his duffle bag.

He opened the door. "Yes?"

A sailor appeared in the doorway. My father was in uniform, and as soon as the sailor saw his rank he saluted. My father returned his salute. I noticed that the sailor was wearing a black armband that said "MP"—he was military police.

"Sorry to disturb you, sir, but we need to speak to Mrs. Betty Braun."

"That's my wife. And why exactly are you looking for her?"

"We have this to pass on to her." The sailor held out an envelope. My father went to take it but the sailor pulled it back. "My orders are this information is for Mrs. Braun only, nobody else." He stepped slightly forward into the cabin, and I saw that there were two other sailors with him. All were wearing side arms and hard expressions.

My mother reached out and took the letter. "Thank you."

"You're welcome, ma'am."

My father went to close the door again and the MP blocked it with his arm. "Sorry, sir, but we aren't here simply to deliver the message. We have orders to facilitate a transfer from the ship."

"What are you talking about?" my father demanded. "If you think you're taking my wife anywhere, you'd better think again!"

"It's not just your wife, sir. You *all* have to accompany us."

"What?"

"It's all right here," my mother said, holding up the letter. "I have to go, and all of you need to come with me."

"Come with you where?" my father asked.

"Wherever these gentleman wish us to be taken."

My father turned to face the sailors.

"We are to accompany you to the destroyer escort *Valiant*, which is stationed off our port side."

"But why?"

"We were not given that information, sir."

"I don't know why," my mother said, "but it's pretty clear from these orders that we do have to go . . . leave this ship."

"Who issued the orders?" my father asked.

"They're from the convoy commander," the sailor said.

My father let out a big sigh. "Fine. Give us fifteen minutes to get packed and we'll go along with you."

"Again, my apologies, sir, but you are to leave with us immediately, and somebody will be coming back to gather up your things."

My father looked angry. I knew how much he hated to be pushed around.

"I guess orders are orders," he finally said. "Excuse me." He turned and walked away, opened a drawer and pulled out his side arm. One of the sailors reached nervously for his revolver as my father slipped his gun into its holster.

"Do your orders include me not being armed?" he asked.

"No, sir."

"Good, then let's get going," my father said. "And gentlemen, I want you to know that I'm not pleased with how this has been handled. As soon as we get aboard the *Valiant* I'm going to have a word with your commanding officer."

"I understand, sir," the sailor said. "It has been rather awkward, sir, and I apologize . . . although it will be getting even more awkward."

"And how is that?" my father asked.

"It's just that once we get aboard the *Valiant*, you *are* our commanding officer, sir."

"What?"

"You have been placed in command of ten Royal Marines, sir."

My father laughed. "I'm in the army, and I'm being put in charge of a group of navy men, Royal Marines?"

"Yes, sir."

"In that case, get out and wait in the hall so we can pack and get ready."

"I'm afraid we can't do that, sir."

"Are you refusing a direct order?"

"No, sir, we are following a direct order. We are to bring you to the ship, and once you are aboard the *Valiant* then you become our commanding officer. I guess that would be the awkward part."

"Do you have any idea what this is about?" my father asked.

"No, sir, I . . . *we* . . . are equally confused. I just hope, sir, that this will not be an issue when you take command, that you won't hold it against us."

My father's expression softened. He walked over and placed a hand on the sailor's shoulder. "I appreciate your dedication to following orders. I'll expect nothing less when I am formally your commanding officer."

"Thank you, sir." He definitely looked relieved!

My father turned to the rest of us. "Well? What are you waiting for? The sooner we get over to the *Valiant*, the sooner we find out what this is all about!"

CHAPTER FOUR

THE MOTOR LAUNCH we were boarding was big, but it seemed so little against the backdrop of the whole Atlantic Ocean. Thank goodness the waves were a bit tamer now.

Along with the three sailors who'd come for us were three more—I guessed they were the crew of the launch. I couldn't help thinking how this boat might have been used to recover survivors from both the sunken cargo ship and the U-boat that sank it. I wondered if any of those German survivors would be on the *Valiant* . . . that made my stomach turn a bit. Although, oddly enough, ever since the letter had come for my mother I hadn't felt a trace of seasickness. Maybe the uncertainty in my head had overcome the unsettledness in my stomach.

The *Valiant* was up ahead, big and grey and all sharp angles, armour and weapons. I'd looked at destroyers longingly in the distance and wondered what it would be like to be aboard one, and now I was going to find out. As we closed in, the ship got bigger and bigger. How were we going to get on board?

The motor launch cut in front of the destroyer and for a split second I thought the big ship was going to slice us in two. The launch went around the port side, made a quick, tight turn and then came right up beside the ship. Attached to the destroyer was a small set of stairs dangling over the side, just above the water. The ship now towered above us while we bobbed up and down beside it.

One of our sailors jumped over to the ship's stairs and tied off one rope, and then a second, securing our launch to the steps. The sailor helped my mother get over the gap and then offered a hand to me and Jack. Our father followed on his own, with the three Marines who had accompanied us.

"Both hands on the railings," a Marine warned me. "We don't want to be fishing you out of the drink."

I didn't need to be told twice. The steps were narrow and slick with spray, and they bounced up and down and side to side as if they were alive. I reached the top and another pair of strong hands pulled me up and onto the deck. There were seven Royal Marines standing there waiting, in two rows.

"Permission to come aboard," my father said.

"Granted, sir," a sailor replied, returning my father's salute.

My father stepped onto the deck. Our three Marines joined the other seven.

"Attention!" one of the Marines yelled.

The two rows came to formal attention.

"Your detachment, sir!" one of them announced.

My father offered a salute, which they all returned. "At ease," he said. "I need to be taken to the captain."

"He is waiting for you in his cabin, sir."

"Lead on."

The original three Marines—along with a fourth— started off. We fell in behind and the rest of the detachment followed. We moved along the deck. Towering above us was the superstructure, the bridge and the guns. They looked so big, so impressive. I knew these were nothing compared to the big guns on a battleship, but still, I couldn't wait to get a closer look at them.

We went in through a big metal hatch and down a corridor. Everything—door, floor, walls and ceiling—was grey metal. There was an echo to our footfalls but no other sounds. Nobody was speaking.

The procession stopped, but I didn't notice quickly enough and bumped into Jack. He scowled at me. It was nice that with everything being so different, so uncertain, so unknown, at least one thing was the same.

The lead Royal Marine knocked on the cabin door.

"Come!"

He opened the door and gestured for us to go in. It was a large space—much bigger than our little cabin on the cargo ship. The captain got to his feet, and he and my father exchanged salutes and then handshakes.

"I'm very pleased to meet you," my father said. "I was hoping you could explain all of this to me . . . to us."

"I was actually hoping you could explain it all to me," the captain replied.

"You don't know?"

"All I know is that I was given very specific orders to bring you all to my ship."

"Who gave those orders?" my father asked.

"They were top priority—from somebody well above my pay grade. I was simply told that you were to be brought here, and *that* was to be turned over to the care of Mrs. Braun." He was pointing to a large object sitting on his desk, covered by a thick blanket. It looked to be rectangular; maybe some kind of box was underneath.

"What is it?" I asked, before I remembered that I shouldn't speak without first being spoken to. "I mean, what is it, sir?"

The captain shook his head. "I only know that it was taken from the sinking U-boat, and it must be very, very important."

We'd seen sailors going into the sinking U-boat. Was that thing under the blanket the reason they'd gone in there?

"Two men lost their lives getting it," the captain said. He paused. "They went down with the U-boat. I hope it was worth it. Captain Braun, you have been given ten members of the Royal Marines to protect it. They will stand guard outside this door. More beds will be brought in here."

"We're going to stay in your cabin?" my mother asked.

"It is the only spot that is suitably private for a woman and children to sleep. Besides, we are under strict orders that you not associate with members of the crew. In fact, we were told to keep your presence on board secret. Did you notice that you encountered no crew other than the members of the guard?"

In the excitement of coming aboard I hadn't really noticed—what was all the secrecy for? This was getting more mysterious by the minute!

"You are to have your meals here and remain in this cabin at all times."

"We can't leave here at all?" Jack asked.

The captain shook his head. "You will not leave this cabin until we reach port, and even then it will be in the dead of night."

"Four days is a long time to be confined to a cabin," my father said.

"Actually, Captain Braun, *you* are free to leave the cabin. And it *would* have been four days, but now we expect to arrive in slightly less than two and a half."

"I didn't realize it would be that soon. I thought the convoy was still four days' sailing from England."

"The convoy will not reach port for four days. But the *Valiant*, along with the corvette *Manchester*, has been ordered to reach port under full steam. In fact, we began to leave the convoy behind the second you stepped aboard."

"Doesn't that leave the convoy at greater risk, lacking the two escort ships?" my father asked.

"Much greater risk."

"But we already got the U-boat," I pointed out.

"Actually, we sank two U-boats tonight . . . so that would leave only about two hundred more still out there. Whatever that . . . *thing* is," he said, again gesturing to the object on his desk, "it has been deemed so valuable that getting it to London as quickly as possible is worth risking the lives of thousands of soldiers and sailors, the ships of this convoy and the hundreds of tons of valuable cargo they're carrying."

We all stared at it as if it were alive.

"And you don't know what it is?" my father asked.

"I have my suspicions, but I have been ordered not to investigate further. In fact, the only people who have seen it at all are me and the Marines who survived the mission to remove it from the U-boat. They are now members of the guard."

"But somebody must know what it is, or none of this would have happened," my father said.

"We used the wireless to send a coded message describing the apparatus. The orders I've outlined are what came back, along with a second set of orders, also on my desk, that are for Mrs. Braun's eyes only. Now, if you'll excuse me, my place is on the bridge."

He closed the door, leaving us alone—alone with that thing under the blanket. We all stared at it, as if it might suddenly disappear or come to life.

"Do you have any idea what it could be?" my father asked.

"They asked specifically for it to be placed in my custody, so I have an idea what it might be," my mother said, "but there's only one way to tell for certain." She walked over and pulled off the blanket. What was underneath was a wooden box about the size of the breadbox on the counter of our old farmhouse.

My mother flipped two clasps and opened it up.

"Oh, my goodness," she gasped. "Do you know what this is?"

There were all sorts of keys with letters on them, and on the top was a series of small light bulbs.

"It looks kind of like a typewriter," I said.

"This is far more than a typewriter," she said. "I never thought I'd see one of these in person." She stopped and looked at us. "If I'm right, this was a communications device for the U-boat."

"So . . . a radio?"

"No, much more important than a radio. This is the device that allowed them to send and receive coded messages. If we can figure how to work this machine, then we can . . ." She paused. "I can't say anything more right now."

"Maybe you should look at your letter," my father suggested as he picked it up.

She took the letter and opened it. "It's in code."

"Well, that's stupid," said Jack. "How are you supposed to know what it says?"

She laughed. "It's bound to be a standard code. I'll be able to translate it fairly quickly. What I do know already is who sent the orders."

"Who?"

"It's signed with one letter, 'G.'"

"It's from G . . . from Little Bill?" I gasped.

"Little Bill" Stephenson was in charge of all British security forces, and his nickname was "God"—or "G" for short—because he seemed to be everywhere and know everything. We'd first met him back at home, when we'd gotten a bit too curious for our own good and stumbled across Camp X, a top-secret training camp for spies. Little Bill certainly had a habit of turning up in our lives when we least expected it—just as he had in Bermuda. And when he did appear, things tended to get pretty exciting for us!

"Do the translation, so we know what it says," my father urged.

Our mother sat down at the captain's desk and opened a drawer, rummaging around for a pen and paper.

"If it's Ireland, I can help you read it," I said.

Ireland was a secret code in which you took the first letter of each of the words, then put them all together to make new words and finally a message.

"Thanks for your offer, dear," she said, "but I'm afraid it might be a little more . . . sophisticated than that."

She started to study the letter.

"Could you show me what code it is so . . . ?"

My father silenced me with a stare. He was right— she needed to concentrate, although she was already so focused on her work that I doubted she'd even heard me. Jack had already sat down on a couch at the far end of the cabin and I went and joined him.

"We're into something, aren't we?" he whispered.

"Something big," I agreed.

"How big do you think it is?"

"Think about it. We're on a destroyer that's left behind a whole convoy, leaving it in danger. This is *huge*."

"You know what the best part is?" Jack asked.

"What?"

"This time, *we* didn't do anything wrong."

He was right. This was one adventure that hadn't

started because of some trouble we'd stupidly got ourselves mixed up in—and that made a nice change. Somehow, though, I was pretty sure we'd end up playing a big part in whatever excitement was about to come.

CHAPTER FIVE

WE WERE TRYING not to stare at our mother as she sat working, a pen in her hand and her head bent over the letter. The surface of the desk was covered with scraps of paper on which she'd written things and then crossed them out. A few of the pages, bunched up noisily, had fallen onto the floor. A couple of them, the tightest balls, rolled along the floor with the motion of the ship.

We were also trying to stay quiet, talking in not much more than whispers, but I got the feeling that Mom wouldn't have flinched even if the ship had been torpedoed. And that was a very real possibility. Why else would they have sent the corvette with us instead of leaving it behind with the convoy? It was here to guard us against a U-boat attack . . . and to take us—and the box, of course—on board if we were sunk.

I had flashbacks to seeing the cargo ship in our convoy going down. I could still see it tilting toward the waves, could still hear the exploding ammunition and the sailors' cries, could still smell the burning fires. It was all so real . . . and so unreal at the same time. So many bizarre, troubling, dangerous things had already happened to me. Sometimes it felt like the only thing that drove one bad thought out of my head was a new bad thought entering.

"Eureka! I think I have it," my mother said.

"That took a long time," Jack said. "You know, nothing personal, but I thought you'd solve it in less than three hours."

"I could have solved it right away if I'd had the crib sheet."

"What's a crib sheet?"

"It tells you how to convert the letters and numbers into the real message. It decodes it. But, of course, it wouldn't make sense to transmit the message and the crib together, or anybody who intercepted the message could read it," she said. "That would really defeat the purpose."

"So how did you decode it without a crib?" I asked.

"Trial and error, basically. I used a series of existing cribs, starting with the most common and working my way through until I found one that worked."

"So . . . what does it say?" my father asked.

"Well, as we knew, it's all about that machine under the blanket. Ironically, if I had one of those machines and Little Bill had one, then we could immediately communicate."

"But I thought it wasn't a radio," I said.

"It isn't, it's a sophisticated encoding and decoding machine. He types his message into his machine and it comes out all gobbledygook. The wireless operator transmits the mixed-up message, which is received by our radio operator. The nonsense message is then typed into our machine, and the original message comes out."

"That's amazing!" I said. "So, with this machine we can read any German messages that we intercept?"

"Well, it's not quite that easy," Mom said. "As I understand it, there are also wheels and rotors within the machine that must be coordinated so that the sending machine and the receiving machine are using the same settings."

"How many wheels are there?" my father asked.

"The message says that there are believed to be three wheels."

"So there are only three ways it can be set?" I asked.

"Not quite. Each wheel probably has multiple settings, so the possible combinations expand exponentially."

"What does that mean?" Jack asked.

"Well, think of the combination lock for your bicycle. It has three little wheels you spin to make the correct combination, right? So, imagine that each number in the combination could only be a 1 or a 2 or a 3. The total number of possible combinations on three wheels with three numbers would be three times three times three, making twenty-seven possibilities."

"Twenty-seven doesn't seem that bad," Jack said.

"Right! But what if each wheel uses ten numbers, 0 to 9, instead of just 1, 2 and 3?" my mother said.

"That's ten times ten times ten, which makes a thousand possibilities."

"That would take a lot longer to figure out by trial and error," I said.

"And what if each wheel has thirty settings? That's thirty times thirty times thirty."

"How many is that?" Jack asked.

"Twenty-seven thousand," my mother and I said in unison.

"I can't get over how you two can do that in your heads," Jack said.

"I can't get over how you *can't* do that in your head," I answered.

"I guess you take after me, Jack," my father said.

"We all have different skills and abilities," my mother pointed out. "It doesn't make one person better or worse."

I wanted to say it *did* make me better than Jack, but I was smart enough to keep my mouth shut and the smirk off my face. My mother had always been good at numbers and patterns. That was why in Bermuda she'd been pulled off her job in the censorship office to work with the decoders searching for secret messages. I'd inherited my mother's ability with numbers—they just made sense to me.

"So the big question," my father said, "is why did they have us brought over to take charge of this thing?"

"Little Bill's letter mentions two reasons," my mother said. "First, we were the only people on the whole convoy who had been sworn to secrecy under the Official Secrets Act. Second, apparently I was the only qualified cryptographer. And on top of that, you'd be able to provide security for the whole thing."

"So we're supposed to babysit this machine until we get to port?" my father asked.

"Not just babysit it. I'm supposed to use the time to try to understand how it works," my mother said.

"Does Little Bill really think you'll figure it out in the next couple of days aboard this ship by yourself?"

"Not figure it out, but at least *start*. He said that these days could mean the difference between life and death for hundreds, or even thousands, of people."

"Really?" Jack asked.

She nodded her head. "Really. So I'd better get started."

Jack was softly snoring, asleep on the couch. My father, on the other hand, was asleep in the captain's bed, and he was snoring like a buzz saw. As for me, I was sitting up in a chair, listening to them and watching my mother. She'd told me to go to sleep a dozen times but I couldn't. It wasn't just that I wasn't tired—I couldn't take my eyes off her and what she was doing. She was studying and tinkering with the mysterious box, fiddling with the dials, opening the back of it, tapping on the keys. Each time she hit a key a different light bulb on the top came on. It was almost hypnotic.

I could tell that she wasn't having a lot of success. It wasn't just her expression, it was also the growing pile of crumpled papers that littered the desk and rolled along the floor as the boat was pushed around by the waves. I got up and walked over.

"So . . . how is it going?"

"It would be going a lot better if this thing had come with an instruction manual."

"But you can figure it out, right?"

She shook her head. "I can solve enough of it to give the experts a head start. It's incredibly complicated, a combination of mechanical and electrical systems. Aside from the keyboard there's a series of plugs, and then there aren't three rotors, but four."

She opened up the back and showed me the four wheels.

"But that makes the code much harder to predict, right?"

"Approximately twenty-six times more difficult, and it was already almost impossible. So, imagine I'm sending a secret message and I'm typing in the words I want encoded. Watch what happens when I push the *A* key."

A bulb on the top lit up—I'd seen that before.

"Now I'll push the same key again," she said. "Watch."

A different light came on.

"If I push the same key ten times, then ten different bulbs light up to signify what letter it will be translated into."

"So if I'm trying to break the code, I can't just use a crib sheet, right?" I said. "Because the first time you type *A* it might come out as a *Z*, but the next time you type it, it could come out as *Q*—is that the idea? It's not going to be the same code all the time."

"That's the basics of it. So two of these machines can

communicate with each other, but only if they're using exactly the same settings so they know how to make sense of the information that's going in."

"But how does the machine do it? I don't understand how that can work," I said.

"I'm starting to. Listen."

My mother put her head close to the box and I did the same. She pushed a button and I heard something move inside the machine.

"Each time I push the key the rotor shifts one position, which sends the electrical current to another lamp and produces a different letter in response."

"Wow. Whoever thought of that was a genius," I said.

"And it will take a genius to sort it all out. Fortunately, there are geniuses waiting for this box when it comes ashore, and it will be turned over to them."

"And that's it for us . . . I mean, for you?"

"I'll definitely have to write a report, but I'm pretty sure that's where my contribution will end."

"Oh . . . that's too bad."

She laughed. "Do you really think you need another adventure?"

"Maybe *need* isn't the right word. I guess you're right," I said.

"On the bright side," she went on, "we'll have plenty of free time to explore England. You know, I've always dreamed of seeing London—Big Ben, the Tower Bridge, the British Museum. Of course, spending time in an air raid shelter was never part of the plan."

I knew what she meant—I'd seen it on the newsreels. Everyone in London knew where their closest air raid shelters were—in tunnels and Tube stations, in basements under factories and schools and hospitals. Many nights the German air force—the Luftwaffe—dropped hundreds of bombs on London and the surrounding area.

For almost a year, during what they called the Blitz, it had gone on every night. That time, thank goodness, had passed, and while there were still bombings they weren't nearly as frequent. With the city being pounded by high explosives, people slept in cots and hammocks in the air raid shelters. I'd been told that the streets in London were filled with rubble from destroyed buildings and homes, and that thousands and thousands of people had been killed and wounded.

Parents sent their children out of the city to get them away from the bombing. Some were sent into the English countryside, but others were shipped to live overseas in places like Canada and Bermuda. It was in Bermuda that we'd met Princess Louise, who had been sent to school there by the English royal family to keep her safe. Of course, safe from the bombing wasn't the same thing as safe from enemy agents. If it hadn't been for Jack and me she would have been kidnapped! We'd saved her. And now here we were, on our way to England to meet her grateful family. At least, that was the plan.

I looked over at my mother sitting there tapping away on that little box and I couldn't help but wonder where it was going to take us. Even the best plans could go off course. We'd sure learned that lesson the hard way!

CHAPTER SIX

THERE WAS A STUFFY, foul smell to the air in the cabin. We had spent more than two days stuck in there, the four of us, eating, sleeping, living in this one little room and bathroom, the only fresh air coming through the tiny porthole. And even then we could only have it open during the day, because at night it had to be closed and covered so that no light would be visible to attract a U-boat's attention. Being jammed in together in close quarters was bothering me, but it was really getting to my father and brother. My father could escape from time to time, but only for short periods, and neither of them did well in confined places. When they weren't

56

eating or sleeping, they were both pacing around the cabin like caged animals. Grouchy, unhappy caged animals.

My mother wasn't pacing—or doing much eating or sleeping, either. She had been practically chained to the machine the whole time. As much as my father and brother wanted out of the cabin, I figured she needed out even more.

The Royal Marine who had brought us our dinner tonight told us we'd make port soon. I would have liked to have gone up on deck to watch as we reached shore, but of course that was out of the question. I just wanted to get on deck and then off this ship and onto solid land.

There was a heavy pounding on the cabin door.

"One minute," my father called out. He turned to my mother. "Cover it up."

My mother didn't seem to hear.

"Betty!" he yelled, and she startled. "Cover the machine up."

She nodded and then closed the wooden cover and pulled the blanket up over the whole thing.

"Come in!" he called out.

One of the sailors in our guard entered and saluted. My father returned the salute.

"We'll be putting you ashore in less than thirty minutes, sir."

"And not a minute too soon," my father said.

"Preparations will be made to move your belongings ashore, sir," he said. "And the team will take possession of and protect the package, sir."

"I think you'll have to come in with weapons drawn if you expect to get it away from my wife."

The sailor looked confused.

"That's a joke, son."

"Oh, yes sir, a good one, sir." He saluted once more and left.

It turned out that my father's little joke wasn't as funny as he'd thought. When it came time to go, my mother in fact refused to allow anybody to take the wooden box from her possession. She claimed that it had been placed in her custody and she wasn't prepared to let it leave her sight until she received very clear orders to do so.

Four Royal Marines—all with side arms and carrying

rifles—led the way. Behind us were two more carrying the box, hidden beneath the blanket, and the final four followed at the rear. Our footfalls echoed off the metal walls of the passage as we made our way to the deck. Walking through the hatch, I took a deep breath of clean, fresh air. It was cool and had been raining so the deck was wet and slick, and I held on to the railing as we walked.

As promised, there were no other sailors present. Not on the ship or on the pier. It was like walking off a ghost ship and into some weird kind of empty, haunted place. This was all part of security. Nobody could be allowed to see us leaving.

We walked down the gangplank. At the bottom sat three vehicles—two army trucks sandwiching a big black car with tinted windows. The platoon stopped right at the car, then the back door opened and a man stepped out.

"Little—"

"Silence!" he ordered. "Say nothing!"

When Little Bill spoke I listened. Everybody listened.

"The Royal Marines who made the discovery are to go in the lead truck while the others get into the rear truck.

The family will travel with me, and the package goes into the car along with us."

Nobody needed to be told twice; everybody scrambled into their assigned vehicles. Little Bill climbed in last and closed the door behind him—once again we were sealed inside. Jack and I were seated facing backward, toward my mother, father and Little Bill. Behind us was a partition that separated the passengers from the driver. The car engine started, followed immediately by the rumbling and fumes of the trucks.

"My apologies for the rude welcome," Little Bill said. "It was important that my name not be mentioned."

"Sorry, I wasn't thinking," I apologized.

"George, I suspect that even in your sleep you're still thinking. Regardless, welcome to England."

"Not quite how I expected to make landfall," my father said.

"I've learned that when your family is involved I should expect the unexpected," Little Bill said. "George and Jack, you didn't actually sink that U-boat yourselves, did you?"

"Of course we . . . oh, you're kidding."

"Bright, George, really bright," my brother said, shaking his head.

"Let me further apologize for interrupting your journey," Little Bill said.

"I think the U-boats did an excellent job of that without your help," my father replied.

"When we came into possession of the package I had to find somebody immediately who could take charge of it," Little Bill said. "There was nobody else in the convoy to whom we could entrust it."

"We appreciate the trust you placed in us."

"I was only half surprised when it turned out you were nearby. I'm starting to think that your boys are like magnets to trouble. It seems to be drawn to them."

"Most of us were asleep when it happened," Jack said.

"Most?" Little Bill asked and turned to me. "Still having sleep problems?"

That was a bit embarrassing. I was hoping he'd forgotten that nightmares were one of the side effects I'd experienced from some of our more . . . let's say *dramatic* adventures.

"Not so bad. It was more about being seasick."

"In that case, when your time in England has come to a close we will arrange for you to fly back to Bermuda."

"In a plane?" I gasped.

"Unless we launch you in a catapult, I believe that is our only option," he joked, and the rest of my family laughed.

"I just meant that I've never been in a plane. That will be amazing."

I'd sat for hours in the harbour in Hamilton, Bermuda, and watched as the Catalina flying boats touched down on the water—those big seaplanes had specially designed hulls so they could land directly on water without using floats. That made them especially useful for search-and-rescue work, and they were pretty good for spotting U-boats, too.

In fact, every plane travelling between Europe and North America stopped in Bermuda to get refuelled. While that was happening, all the letters and packages they were carrying were taken ashore, opened, scanned for secret messages and then put back on board with nobody the wiser. That was the job my mother did, searching for secret messages, codes or microdots—important information photographed and shrunk down to a micro-scopic size.

"I think we'd all enjoy a flight back," my mother said.

"It's the least we can do, especially considering the extent to which we're going to have to impose further on your free time," Little Bill said.

"Further?" my mother asked.

"I'm going to have to request that your family continue to accompany the package, and I'd like you all to be debriefed," he explained.

"Does this mean I'm not going to see Louise?" Jack asked, a bit nervously.

This was a new side to my brother—the lovesick teenager—but I'd already learned the hard way that my parents did not find it as funny as I did. I'd have to wait and tease him later.

"Of course you'll see her," Little Bill said. "Arrangements have been made, and we would not willingly disappoint any members of the royal family. The meeting will just be slightly delayed."

"How slightly?" Jack asked.

"That has not yet been determined. Perhaps you'll

end up staying in England a little longer. That might give you time to see even more of your friend," Little Bill said.

"That would be gr— That would be . . . um . . . fine!" Jack was trying not to let on just how happy he would be to have more time with Louise. Not teasing him was just about killing me now!

"So where exactly are we going?" I asked.

"I should have expected you to get down to business, George. We are going to Bletchley Park."

"Bletchley!" my mother exclaimed.

"I'm not surprised you've heard of it," Little Bill said. "What exactly *have* you heard?"

My mother looked embarrassed, as though she'd been caught with her hand in the cookie jar.

"Well, not much, really. It's just that I've heard rumours, little tidbits, about it being the headquarters for encryption operations."

"It certainly is where most of our encryption work is undertaken, but the place itself might not be quite so grand as the word 'headquarters' suggests. You'll see for yourself."

"I'm *so* looking forward to it," my mother said. "Bletchley Park . . . can you believe it, boys?"

"I was hoping for Buckingham Palace," Jack muttered.

"I imagine you'll be visiting there, or possibly Windsor Castle, depending on the bombings," Little Bill said.

"I thought they'd subsided," my father said.

"Subsided but not stopped. The Luftwaffe's bombing runs are not as frequent but they are still just as deadly. The bombing of Birmingham two nights ago resulted in over three hundred deaths."

"That's awful," my mother said.

"I didn't realize they could be that deadly," I added.

"They can be even more devastating, but those facts are generally not released to the public," Little Bill said. "We'd rather the Germans not find out exactly how damaging their bombs have been, and beyond that it's bad for civilian morale. Of course, you four are often privy to classified information . . . which I know you will keep completely confidential. This little box, for example," he said, tapping it. "This is beyond top secret, this is *ultra* secret."

"You needn't worry about me letting any important

information slip," my father said. "As far as I can make out, it's nothing more than a fancy typewriter."

"With all the keys in the wrong places," Jack added.

"Hopefully Mrs. Braun now has a more sophisticated understanding of its workings?"

"I have some rudimentary thoughts. It was helpful to have George to bounce ideas off."

Little Bill turned to me again. "I want to hear what you all have to say in the debriefing, and then I need you never to say another word about it. This little box is going to save tens of thousands of lives, and your silence is absolutely crucial to its work."

"You know you don't have to worry about us," Jack said. "Loose lips sink ships."

"Truer words have never been spoken," Little Bill said. Then he leaned across the seat toward the blanket-covered box. "Shall we unwrap our present?" he asked.

Once he had removed the blankct and then opened up the top, he said, "It certainly looks like the standard Enigma machine."

"Enigma?" Jack asked.

"That is the name of the encrypting system that the Germans use."

"So you've seen one of these before?" I asked.

"We have a number of models, but this is the first of the new naval machines we have ever captured. With this machine we will hopefully be able to track and destroy the U-boats. And the implications of that fact . . . well, it would be nearly impossible to overstate the importance of being able to safeguard the convoys that are bringing troops, munitions, all manner of absolutely crucial supplies across the ocean to Europe. So far we've been losing this contest in the Atlantic, and losing could mean losing the entire war. This machine that you have been studying could finally turn the tide in our favour."

The car fell into silence as we all stared at the box. Riding along with us was the key to winning the war.

CHAPTER SEVEN

THE CAR HIT another bump and I bounced up from my seat. We'd traded the stale air and rolling seas of the ship's cabin for the stale air and rough roads of the car. The driver had cranked down the tinted window a couple of inches, but other than that we were sealed inside, invisible to the outside world, just as Little Bill had insisted.

The vehicle slowed down and we made a turn.

"We're here," Little Bill announced.

I turned around so that I could see through the little opening in the partition that separated the passengers from the driver and the front windshield. We were driving down a lane. On one side was a pond, woods to the other, and up ahead was a checkpoint—guards with rifles, sandbags and a small hut. Beyond that loomed a large old building.

We slowed down as we approached the guards but didn't stop. They must have known who we were because they just waved us through. As we got closer I could see the building more clearly. It was big and tall with parts that looked almost like turrets, but instead of a castle it reminded me of a mansion—maybe a haunted mansion from a ghost story. That impression didn't last long because I soon saw that the place was bristling with activity: lots of people walking, talking in groups, whizzing around on bicycles, moving everywhere.

The car came to a stop, then the door popped open from the outside and a guard was standing there.

"Welcome to Bletchley," Little Bill said.

My parents climbed out, and Jack pushed me aside to exit next. Once I was out Little Bill followed, carrying the machine, which had been seated beside me the whole way.

He called out to two men standing by the building's front door. "Gentlemen, please."

They walked over. I thought he was going to introduce us but I was wrong.

"Get this to Hut 8, immediately."

"Oh, my goodness," one of them said. "Is this . . . ?"

"Shark."

"No, seriously," one of them said.

"Shark," Little Bill repeated.

Their expressions changed from disbelief to shock to glee. They started jumping up and down excitedly like a couple of kids on Christmas morning.

Gently, almost lovingly, one of them took the box from Little Bill.

"Don't drop it," the other said.

"Of course I won't drop it. Do you think I'm daft?"

"Not daft, just not very coordinated. I've seen you with a rugby ball."

"My hope is that nobody is going to try to tackle me between here and Hut 8."

"Gentlemen, please, make sure you give it to Alan."

They started off, the two of them holding it together.

"We'll go to the Hut ourselves, but first things first. It's time for tea," said Little Bill.

We sat in the dining hall. A line of people with trays waited to select their food from serving dishes placed on tables all along the side of the room. We didn't have to line up, though. Instead, a young girl—not much older than I was—came over with a little tea trolley and left it at our table. I wanted to ask her how old she was, but that didn't seem polite. Besides, I always hated it when people asked my age. I was too old for that to feel anything but condescending.

Hundreds of people were there for their morning tea break, and their enthusiastic conversations and noisy clinking of cutlery were punctuated by bursts of laughter.

"How many times have we shared a pleasant cup of tea together?" Little Bill asked as he poured.

"I'm not sure how many times, but it's often not been this pleasant," I answered, reaching for one of the sweets from the trolley.

He smiled. Without asking he dropped in three cubes of sugar and then added milk before handing me my cup of tea.

"Thank you, sir."

"Pleasure."

He continued to fix everybody's tea. He didn't need to ask what they wanted. He never forgot anything. Little Bill had a photographic memory, and details, even those as trivial as what we took in our tea, were lodged in his head right alongside the details of the activities of thousands of spies, agents and secret missions and bases spread across two continents. And this important man was having tea with ordinary old us—again!

"You must be curious about this place," Little Bill said.

"Curious, but smart enough to know you're not going to tell us much," Jack said.

"Perhaps I'll simply confirm what you already know. This station is dedicated to the decoding of enemy messages."

"Are all these people here to break codes?" I asked.

"You are seeing only a small percentage of the thousands of people necessary to make this station function."

"But are all of them code breakers?" I asked.

"They are all part of the *process* needed to break codes, but only a small percentage perform that specific work. It requires a very unique and unusual type of person. We are always struggling to get enough people who can master the craft." He paused. "I would guess that if you were old enough you might in fact be working here, George."

"That girl pushing the tea trolley wasn't much older than me," I said.

"I suspect that she is closer to Jack's age than yours. There are many positions—serving tea, delivering messages, helping with the day-to-day running of the place—in which young people can make a contribution."

"Sort of like what we were doing at the Princess Hotel," Jack said.

"Exactly."

The Princess Hotel was the station in Bermuda where all letters and packages were searched as they travelled between North America and Europe. As well, radio messages from U-boats and German ships were intercepted there. Both Jack and I had worked at the hotel doing odd jobs, ranging from mopping floors to emptying garbage cans. At least until we'd stopped those Nazi agents from kidnapping Louise. After that, we weren't even allowed at the hotel. It was a strange way to say thank you for foiling a Nazi plot, but our mother had decided she'd finally had enough of her boys being spies.

"And due to the nature of their work here, all of these people, including the young girl pushing the tea trolley, have taken an oath under the Official Secrets Act, just as you have, not to share any information they learn while acting in service to the government. In fact, Bletchley Park employees are forbidden even to acknowledge that they work here."

"You know we won't talk about anything," I said.

"I didn't even feel a need to mention that," Little Bill said. "Although right now I do need you all to talk. Betty, I'm going to have you brought to Hut 8 to meet with the men who are ultimately going to break the codes associated with that machine."

"And Shark is going to help break the naval codes," I said.

"As soon as I mentioned its code name, I knew you'd picked it up," Little Bill said. "Yes, while this is an Enigma machine, Shark is the code name for the key specific to the U-boats." He got that thoughtful look again. "George, you were assisting your mother, so perhaps you could go with her to Hut 8 and add your two cents' worth to the debriefing."

"And me and my father?" Jack asked.

"You will both be debriefed as well, and then I'm going to ask for your father's expertise, if I may."

"Of course," my father said. "You know we're always happy to offer whatever help we can."

"Excellent. I was hoping that you would meet with the head of security and do a brief walk-through of the security measures here at Bletchley."

"My pleasure," my father said. "On the way in I did notice a bank of anti-aircraft guns, and I saw at least two tanks in the woods on the other side of the pond."

"I didn't see any of that," Jack said.

"When you spend two years stationed in North Africa facing Rommel and his Panzer units, you learn to notice tanks."

"It would be most interesting for you to go and *examine* those tanks up close," Little Bill said.

His slight emphasis on the word "examine" made me wonder. One thing I'd learned about Little Bill was that he often said what he didn't mean, and didn't say what he really meant. Not that he lied to us, but sometimes his real meaning wasn't exactly obvious. What was he getting at this time?

Just then an old man, all bent over, came toward us pushing a trolley piled high with dirty dishes. It looked as though he was really struggling. How old was he? The man made the Home Guard back in Canada look like spring chickens.

"Are you almost finished?" he asked. There was a quaver in his voice.

Before anybody could answer he started clearing away the dishes. He took Jack's cup—still half full—right out of his hand. Jack looked shocked.

"It's important to keep things tidy," the old man said. "Some people have no manners." Then he turned to our mother. "Did you raise these boys with manners?"

"We certainly tried, although not always with the best results."

The old man cackled like a goose . . . that laugh sounded awfully familiar . . . I looked more closely at him, straight into his eyes. I could never forget those eyes.

"Ray?"

The old man smiled and straightened up.

"I didn't know if I could fool good old Georgie!" he said.

CHAPTER EIGHT

"RAY, WHAT ARE you doing here?" I asked.

"Everybody has to be somewhere," he said. "Shame my costume didn't fool you."

"It sure fooled me," Jack said.

"I wouldn't have recognized you in a million years," my father added.

"Yes, it is . . . *good*," my mother said icily.

It was no secret that she wasn't fond of Ray. She thought he was a bad influence on me, and I guess I couldn't really argue. After all, he was a convicted thief and safecracker who had taught me how to pick locks—as well as a magician, master of disguise and now an agent working for the government. She'd been pleased when he suddenly disappeared from Bermuda three months ago without a goodbye. I'd been wondering ever since if he was okay and hoping nothing bad had happened to him—in the spy business, when someone disappeared it was considered bad form to ask questions.

"It might be a good costume, but it didn't fool George. What gave me away?" Ray asked.

"The laugh. I recognized your laugh."

"I'll have to work on that."

"And then I looked at your eyes," I said. "It's like you once said to me, you can't disguise somebody's eyes."

"You really are a fine student, a quick study," Ray said. "Oh, by the way, does anybody want to buy this?" He held out a watch.

"Hey, that's mine!" Jack yelled as he snatched it back from Ray.

"No need to be rude, Jack," Ray said. "Let's call it a gift from me to you. After all, it's not like you have any money."

Jack looked confused—then he checked his pocket where his wallet should have been.

Ray reached into his own pocket and tossed the wallet to Jack. "I'm afraid old habits die hard," he said.

"So, as you might have surmised, Ray has not lost his touch, and he has been reassigned to Bletchley," Little Bill explained.

"You're breaking codes?" I asked.

"Me? No, it's a different type of bird who does that, and believe me they are *very* different. I'm here working on deception and camouflage."

"It looks like you're playing dress-up," Jack said.

"Costumes are a very small part of things. Maybe I'll have the opportunity to show you . . . assuming I'm allowed."

"I'll have a word with the station chief," Little Bill said. "I think you can at least share some of the basics of your work here."

"That would be wonderful! You know how I like to show off!"

"In the meantime, would you do me a favour? Could you bring Betty and George to Hut 8 and introduce them to Alan?"

Ray's face took on a funny expression. "I'll bring them

there, but there's no guarantee Alan will be there, or that he'll talk to them if he is. You know how he can be."

Little Bill nodded. He obviously knew what Ray meant—now *I* wanted to know.

"Excellent. Captain, Jack, I will be your guide," Little Bill said.

My father and Jack set off with Little Bill. As for me, I was curious to meet this "Alan" fellow. What was he going to be like?

"I was more than a little shocked to see your family here," Ray said to my mother. "Have you been assigned to Bletchley?"

"Goodness no, we're just in England for a short visit."

"Well, Bletchley Park is not a typical sightseeing destination," Ray said, "but I imagine you can't tell me more, so I won't ask."

We followed Ray out of the dining hall and through some rooms. It was a large, rambling place that looked like it was once a family home but had been converted for military use.

"We came to England to meet Louise's family," I explained.

"This ain't exactly Buckingham Palace or Windsor Castle," Ray said, gesturing around. I could see his point—there were people sitting at desks or rushing about with boxes and file folders and what looked like bits of machines. It looked more like a cross between a business office and a rundown building than a royal residence.

"We got a little diverted," my mother said. I could tell by her tone of voice that she didn't want the discussion of our plans to go much further.

"But this place is big," I said. "Sort of like a castle."

"Oh, it's a funny old place all right, a bit of a dog's breakfast of different building styles. The people here called it 'the Victorian Monstrosity' even before all the new buildings started going up on the lawns. Those huts are sprouting up like mushrooms."

We followed Ray as he led us through a maze of corridors and hallways.

"So what are you doing here besides serving tea?"

"I hope I'll be able to show you. I've been pulling some rabbits out of my hat since I got assigned here," Ray said.

"You're doing magic?" I asked.

"In a manner of speaking. A good conjuror has many tricks up his sleeve."

"I imagine that would be helpful if we wanted to entertain the enemy with card tricks and make coins appear and disappear," my mother said.

"It's not so much coins and cards as tanks and battleships and whole airfields."

"That I'd pay to see," I said.

"You've already seen some of it," Ray said. "Ask your father to tell you about those tanks he's going out to inspect."

My mother gave him a questioning look, but I thought I knew.

"Are you saying they aren't really there?" I asked.

"Oh, they're there, your father saw them. The real question is, are they real?"

"My husband has seen a good many tanks in his time," my mother said. "He fought in North Africa, so he would know a real tank from a fake."

"I'm sure he would, if he took a good close look," Ray said. "We have to hope that never happens when we set out to fool the enemy, because our work is based on illusions, impressions and assumptions. We try to make a whole lot of things look real when they aren't, or look like something else, or disappear entirely."

"And that's what you do here?" I asked.

"That's the whole aim of the Prop Shop," Ray said. "I'm going to see if I can get permission for you to see it. You know what a showman I am. All this secrecy stuff is making me crazy! It would be nice to show it off to you before you leave . . . when are you leaving?"

"Very soon," my mother said. "We just have to be debriefed and then we're off."

"Things don't exactly operate with military precision around here," Ray said, "so don't expect anything to happen quickly."

We exited through a door and we were at the back of the main building. Ahead of us was a stretch of lawn occupied by several small wooden buildings. A forest stretched out behind that. Each of the buildings was connected to the main building by a small gravel path, and each was equipped with blackout shutters, now open to allow sunlight in.

"All the huts look pretty much alike," Ray said. "You have to know which is which to find your way around."

"Wouldn't it be easier to just put up signs?" I asked.

"No signs here, or anywhere in all of England, for that matter."

"I don't understand."

"They took down all the street and road signs so that if you don't know where you're going you can't get there," he said.

"But why would they do that?" I asked.

"You don't want to make it any easier for invaders. Even if it's just a dozen or so German commandos who are put ashore by a U-boat, or who drop in out of the sky. You don't want them to be able to get around easily."

Instinctively I looked up—nothing but clear blue sky with a few fluffy, innocent-looking clouds.

"This place is pretty secure, but still, it's like Churchill said about our island home: *We shall fight on the beaches, we shall fight on the landing grounds, we shall fight in the fields and in the streets . . .*"

Even though I'd heard those words a dozen times

before they still sent a shiver up my spine. I also knew what came next. "*We shall never surrender,*" I said.

"You got that right," Ray said. "No surrender, no retreat. Whether we're fighting invaders, or the spies and enemy sympathizers who are sending back reports."

"Spies are bad enough, but I really can't understand sympathizers," I said. "How could anybody be sympathetic to the Nazis and betray their own people?"

"I suppose they could have their reasons. You might even feel a bit sorry for some of them, if you knew," Ray said.

I laughed out loud. "After what we've been through, I don't think I could ever feel sorry for any traitor."

"Well, sometimes people get threatened or tricked," Ray said.

That seemed like such a funny thing to say. Instantly, the suspicious, "see a spy behind every bush" part of me wondered if Ray was saying something more.

"Here we are," he said. "Hut 8." He pulled open the door and gestured for us to go in. My mother led and I was right on her heels.

The room was filled with desks and chairs, the walls

were lined with chalkboards, and there was a huddle of men at the far end—I figured that the Enigma machine was at the centre of their attention. They were so focused that they didn't even seem to notice us come in.

"Hey, Professor!" Ray called out.

The men stopped talking and turned to face us. The group parted slightly, allowing the man at the centre to emerge.

"Yes?" he asked. He was wearing a suit jacket and pyjama bottoms. His face was unshaved and his hair went wildly in a dozen directions.

"This is the person who brought you your new toy," Ray said.

The man's eyes widened and he walked toward us.

"Professor, this is Betty Braun and her son George."

"You brought us the Shark?" the man asked, pointing at the machine. His voice was high-pitched, almost squeaky.

"We were assigned to bring it to you, and I started the analysis," my mother said.

"Come, tell . . . show us," he said.

My mother stepped forward and was almost surrounded by the group of men, leaving Ray and me on the outside. She started to talk, and they began to pepper her with questions and comments.

"I'm not even sure they're speaking English," Ray said. "And they're certainly not writing it." He gestured to the blackboards, which were covered with letters, numbers and symbols, all with boxes drawn around them and with arrows connecting the boxes. I couldn't make heads or tails out of it.

"And the part that *is* in English doesn't make any sense whatsoever," Ray said, pointing to another board.

This time I saw words, but Ray was right—they were unusual and put together in nonsensical sentences.

"These are the most peculiar people I've ever met," Ray said under his breath. "And believe me, I've met some very unusual people in my time."

I couldn't stop myself from laughing. Ray *was* just about the most unusual person I'd ever met.

"Okay, I know, I know, who am I to talk about being a little different?"

"You are one of a kind, Ray," I said.

"And this coming from a twelve-year-old spy?" he asked.

"I'm hardly a spy. I just stumbled into things."

"You didn't stumble into anything," Ray said. "You're as extraordinary as these people, just in a different way. Now, I have to get going, I have work to do." He started off.

"Ray!" I called out, and he stopped and turned around. "Will I see you again before we leave?"

He nodded his head. "I have a suspicion you'll see a lot more of me . . . because I also have a suspicion you're not leaving quite yet."

CHAPTER NINE

OUR FAMILY MET UP again in the dining hall for our evening meal, where we were joined by the commander at Bletchley, whose name was Edward Travis. Little Bill wasn't able to join us—he sent his apologies, but he had important work to do. I imagined he'd be spending the evening in Hut 8 with the Professor, and I was pretty sure the Professor wouldn't be sleeping at all that night, even if he *was* in his pyjamas.

Afterward we were shown to the small guest cottage for overnight visitors at Bletchley. It was no more than a five-minute walk from the mansion. In the morning we'd be escorted to the train and taken down to London. I guessed I wasn't going to be seeing Ray again after all, although he did seem to have a way of popping up when least expected. In some ways he was like a magic trick himself, a living illusion.

My father and brother couldn't stop talking about what they'd seen. After their debriefing, they'd been taken to see the tanks—fake tanks, as it turned out, and artillery pieces made out of canvas and wood. They said that up close it was obvious they weren't real, but from a distance, for example from an airplane, they would have fooled anybody, including my father. Those were some of the props that Ray and the Prop Shop were working on. Really they were nothing but an illusion, a magic trick, and who better than Ray to fool people?

My mother had been remarkably quiet, as if she was completely preoccupied, or completely exhausted. Or maybe it was a combination of the two. She hadn't been sleeping well ever since we'd boarded the ship, and basically not at all since we'd been given possession of the Enigma machine. Tonight she'd be able to sleep. At least, I hoped so.

"Maybe we should all turn in," my mother suggested. "It's getting late."

"I'm all for that," Jack agreed. "The sooner we go to bed, the sooner we can get up and leave."

"And the sooner you can see *a certain special somebody*," I joked.

"You're going to be seeing stars if you don't shut your—"

"Jack," my mother warned him. "Nobody will be threatening anybody." She turned to me. "Or teasing anybody. Agreed?"

"Sure, I wouldn't want to stand in the way of—"

There was a knock on the door and we all jumped.

"I'll get it," my father said.

When he stood up I noticed that he was still wearing his service revolver. He undid the clasp on the holster and placed his hand on the butt of the gun, ready to remove it if need be. Maybe I wasn't the only one who'd become more careful—or even a little paranoid. He walked over to the door, but stood slightly off to one side. I didn't need to ask why he did that—if somebody shot through the wooden door it wouldn't hit him. How strange that he—and I—would think that way. There was another knock.

"Who is it?" he asked.

"Bill, Little Bill."

I recognized the voice—there was no question it was him.

My father opened the door.

"Sorry for calling so late," Little Bill said, "but I needed to speak to you, and I'll be gone before the morning."

It was a safe bet that he wasn't just here to say goodbye.

"First, I'd like to thank all of you for taking a slight detour in your travels."

"It was both our duty and a pleasure," my father said.

"Just to see this place and to meet the code breakers was a highlight for me," my mother added.

"What did you think of the Professor?"

"He is a genius," my mother said.

"Is he the guy who was wearing his pyjamas?" Jack asked. I'd mentioned that little detail to him.

"Please don't confuse his attire, or his lack of social graces, with his contributions. Through his work here at

Bletchley, he has done more to turn the war in our favour than almost any other individual. He *is* a genius."

"I've never met a genius before," I said. And I'd never imagined one in pyjamas before.

"I don't use that word lightly. I've known many people who are brilliant, but he is more than that. He sees things that nobody else can see. That's what makes him able to break codes that others think are unbreakable."

"He is very, very impressive," my mother said.

"He was also impressed with you. Apparently he said some very nice things about you to Edward Travis."

"That was very sweet of him."

"And then Edward came to speak to me," Little Bill said. "And that is why I'm here. Edward asked me questions, not only about you, Betty, but about your entire family. He has asked a favour of me, which is really a favour of your family."

I was positive I knew where this was going.

"Does he want my mother to work here?" I asked.

"More than that, he wants to know if *all* of you can work here, assigned on a temporary basis for the summer."

"All of us?" my father asked.

"All four of you," Little Bill said. "Your wife would be assigned to Hut 8 to work with Alan on breaking the Shark code. You, Captain, would take on responsibility in assessing, testing and revamping security."

"And he wants us, too?" Jack asked.

"He has *very* specific tasks in mind for you and George."

There was a tone to his voice that sent a chill up my spine.

"Tasks? Like . . . ?" Jack asked.

"You two will be delivering mail, relaying messages, pushing the tea trolley about and doing odd jobs around the compound," Little Bill said.

"But there's more to it than that, right?" I asked.

He nodded. "As always, George, you are one step ahead of the game. This facility is perhaps the most important station we have. It must be protected against spies, saboteurs and sympathizers."

"Do you believe it has been compromised or infiltrated?" my father asked.

"We have no evidence that it has, but it might just be that we haven't imagined or investigated all the possibilities for subterfuge. We must always be vigilant and aware."

"And that's what you want us to do while we're delivering mail and serving tea and doing odd jobs," I said.

"Doing those tasks, you would be able to move freely from department to department, location to location, within Bletchley. Nobody knows who you are, and, as Ray so aptly pointed out, your innocence places you boys in a unique position to put your special talents to work here."

"You want our boys to become spies *again?*" my mother asked.

"Not spies. Observers."

"I thought we'd agreed not to put our boys at risk anymore," my father said.

"The risk would be minimal. They would operate here within the confines of Bletchley, under your care and supervision," Little Bill told our parents. "And, as I said to Commander Travis, this would be done only with your complete knowledge and permission."

"Would that mean I wouldn't get to see Louise and her family?" Jack asked.

"Obviously you wouldn't be leaving tomorrow for

London. But Louise and her family are only a short ride away. I would imagine that you'd see even more of her while you're here over the next two months than you would have during the shorter, planned trip."

"Then I'm in," Jack said.

"Me too," I quickly added.

"Do either of you two think you actually have a vote in this decision?" my father asked.

"No, sir," I said.

"We know it's up to you," Jack agreed. "We were just saying we'd be willing, that is, if you let us."

My mother and father looked at each other.

"It would be rather exciting to be part of what's happening here," my mother said. "It would be quite the learning experience, and a chance to contribute to the war effort."

"It would be a significant contribution," Little Bill said. "And it would be temporary—your positions in Bermuda would await your return."

Slowly my father shook his head. "This might not be a democracy, but I still think I'm outvoted. Okay, we're in."

CHAPTER TEN

JACK AND I STOOD on the lawn facing the front entrance to the main building at Bletchley. It was early morning, and there was a rush of people in and out as the night shift ended and the day shift began. We were all going to start work today—our mother in Hut 8, our father with the security detail, Jack in maintenance, and I'd be joining another girl, a couple of years older than me, delivering mail, messages, parcels and urns of tea to the different departments.

"Just don't screw this up," Jack said.

"Don't *you* screw it up," I replied.

"I'm not the one who sees spies behind every bush and potted plant."

"Yeah? Well, don't forget, so far I've been *right*!" I said. "Besides, that's what we're here for, isn't it? To find spies?"

"Just because we're looking doesn't mean there's anything here to find," Jack said. "It's like Little Bill said— they don't have any evidence that anything or anyone is doing wrong here."

"So I'll just keep my eyes open."

"And your mouth shut. If you do something stupid and we get sent home early I'm not going to be happy. And believe me, if I don't stay happy, *you're* not going to stay happy, or *unhurt*."

"Are you looking for a fistfight right here on the lawn?" I asked.

"If it was me and you it wouldn't be much of a fight."

"Okay, big man, act brave while you still can."

"And what is that supposed to mean?" Jack asked.

"Mom and Dad have both told me that I'm bigger at twelve than you ever were. It won't be long until I'm just as big as you, or bigger."

"It doesn't make any difference. You'll always be my *little* brother."

"Younger, yes. Littler, maybe not for much longer. You'd better treat me nice now and hope I have a good memory."

"You've still got a long way to go, *baby* brother," Jack said, patting me on the head. "So maybe you'd better treat *me* nice right now, and that means not fouling things up here and making it so I can't see Louise."

"Sure, whatever, you'll probably get to see her . . . for all the good it's going to do you. Don't forget, she's royalty and you're just a commoner," I said.

"Not as common as you. Remember, just keep your mouth shut and your eyes open for anything unusual."

Just then, a man wearing a gas mask pedalled by us on a bicycle. I couldn't see his face but I certainly recognized the pyjamas.

"Of course, around here you'd have to be pretty strange to qualify as 'unusual,'" I said.

"Is that the man from the hut?" Jack asked.

I nodded. "That's the Professor, Mom's new boss, the genius."

"You'd figure a genius could remember to change out of his pyjamas."

"He probably has other things on his mind."

"So should we. I'll see you after work. And remember, eyes open, mouth shut!"

I made a zippering motion across my mouth and opened my eyes in an exaggerated way. In spite of himself Jack laughed, and then he walked off toward the maintenance hut, leaving me alone on the lawn.

It was time for me to get to work too. I took a deep breath and walked through the door to report for duty.

The main atrium was crowded and loud and people rushed in every direction. There were lots of nods and waves, handshakes and back slaps. I was trying to find Room 1030. I'd been told it was along the corridor to the right. I followed the hall and looked at the numbers above the doors until I came to the right one. I knocked on the door.

"Come." It was a woman's voice.

I opened the door. "Hello, I'm—"

"You're *late* is what you are," the woman said. She was sitting behind a desk, the top of which was covered in stacks of papers. She had a scowl on her face—one that I had a strange feeling was permanent.

"Sorry, I was just a little—"

"There is no room for excuses or apologies or tardiness," she said. "Do you plan on being late for every shift?"

"No, ma'am, I plan on never being late again . . . ever . . . for anything."

"I will be holding you to that. I am Mrs. Pruitt. I will be your supervisor. Now sit."

There was only one chair that wasn't piled high with folders, so I sat there.

"You have been told to report for work here because your parents have been assigned to work at Bletchley. Is that correct?"

"Yes, ma'am."

"And what exactly do you know about Bletchley?"

"Not much," I lied. "Just what I've been told by Mr. Travis."

"*Mr.* Travis? Are you referring to *Commander* Travis?"

"Yes, of course."

"Perhaps things are a little less formal in the colonies,"

she said, "but here you will address all supervisors, superiors and seniors by their formal titles and all military officers by their rank."

"Yes, Mrs. Pruitt."

She looked pleased . . . well, at least not so angry.

"I assume that Commander Travis has informed you of both the importance and secret nature of this station. You will be required to sign an oath under the Official Secrets Act—"

"I've already signed it."

"And do you understand what it means?" she asked.

"I cannot talk about anything that I see or hear."

"To anybody. Ever."

"I understand, ma'am."

"Good. You must also understand that what you are doing is vital to the war effort. You will be delivering letters and parcels that pertain directly to combat operations. As such, your failure to execute your tasks may result in lives being lost."

"Yes, ma'am."

"I understand that you've had similar responsibilities in other facilities, although it is rather difficult for me to understand how somebody of your age could come with previous experience."

"I have had experience in two different facilities," I said. I had worked at the station in Bermuda that searched for enemy messages, and also delivering letters to prisoners of war at Camp 30 in Bowmanville. "Of course, I can't tell you about where they were or what I was doing."

"Nor would I expect you to. For now, despite your *extensive* experience, you will be under the direct supervision of another person . . . somebody with more knowledge of our procedures. Her name is Sally, and she is *so* much older than you. I believe she will be *fifteen* on her next birthday."

I wondered if this was the girl I had already seen in the cafeteria. There couldn't be too many kids working around here.

"You will report immediately to her in the mailroom and begin your rounds."

"Yes, ma'am." I stood up and offered her my hand. "It was a pleasure to meet you."

Her expression softened and I got the feeling she was almost on the verge of cracking a smile.

CHAPTER ELEVEN

I TRAILED ALONG behind Sally as we walked and talked. Actually, she talked and I listened. She was very friendly and incredibly talkative. If keeping your mouth shut was part of the job, she was failing miserably. She certainly wasn't giving away any earth-shaking secrets, but she was making idle conversation—with *everybody* we passed.

"Do you know everyone who works here?" I asked.

"I don't know if anybody knows everybody. There are thousands of people working at Bletchley, and new people are coming all the time."

"But everybody says hello to you."

"I think that's more because of my job. Because I go to all the different offices and buildings, I get to meet people. But a lot of the people here work on just one tiny part of the operation and they stay in one place. So the people in Hut 3 don't seem to know the people who work next door in Hut 4."

"Is that because they're all so busy? Don't they meet each other over meals in the dining hall?" I asked.

"Yes, they're really busy, and because everything is so secret nobody wants to talk to anybody else except to say good morning or good night. Or, I don't know, maybe they talk about the weather?"

That was good to know, but it would certainly make my job harder.

"I've only been here a little while, but already I've seen some pretty odd characters. I bet you've got some good stories." Maybe I could get her to give me a rundown on who to keep an eye on.

She laughed. "My mother—she works in the cafeteria—she says it's a strange mix here. There are university math professors, chess masters, actors, writers, magicians and 'girls in pearls.'"

"Girls in pearls?"

"The upper class. Lots of the women here are from high society, even members of the royal family, if you can believe that."

We made another turn, through a door that was unmarked, cut through the kitchen and then went out to the back of the building.

We had already been in five of the huts, including the one where my mother and the Professor worked. They were all pretty well identical, occupied by code breakers who were assigned to different specific tasks. One hut worked on army radio traffic, another focused on the Luftwaffe—the German air force—while yet another concentrated on the navy. That navy code was named Dolphin, while Hut 8 was now working exclusively on Shark, the U-boat code.

We'd been told all of this by Little Bill, but I didn't actually know how much Sally knew. We both knew we weren't supposed to talk about what went on inside each building.

"And of course there are so many people who are not only different but from different places," Sally said.

"Scots, Welsh, Kiwis, Aussies, Polish and French, and lately you Americans have been here."

"I'm not an American, I'm a Canadian!"

"You both sound the same to me with your cute little accents."

"First off, I don't have an accent and . . ." I realized how stupid that sounded since we all have accents. "I don't have an *American* accent. How would you like it if I said you had an Irish accent?"

"Well, that would be ridiculous. I'm obviously *English*."

"And I'm obviously *Canadian*."

"I didn't know you Canadians were so *sensitive*," she said.

"And I didn't know you English were so *smug* and *insensitive*."

She didn't look too pleased with me. Not a good idea on my part to pick a fight with somebody I needed to have as a friend.

"Look, we're all on the same side. If you think about it, isn't this whole war we're fighting because one group of people thinks they're better than all the other groups?" I asked.

"Yes . . . I just never thought of it that way." She bowed slightly. "My apologies to a Canadian."

"And mine if I offended an Englishwoman." I did a small curtsey and she started laughing.

"No offence, but that curtsey was a dead giveaway that you're a colonial. Of course you're a boy so you should have bowed, silly, but if you *were* to curtsey it would look more like this." She did a graceful curtsey. "Now, we'd better get moving. If Mrs. Pruitt sees us lollygagging or even laughing she'll become very unpleasant."

"I have trouble picturing her *not* being unpleasant. Does her scowl actually get scarier?"

"Oh, much, much scarier, believe me, and you don't want to see it."

I was glad that Sally knew where she was going, because all the huts looked the same to me. "You know, this place is like a maze. Do you ever get lost?"

"Not so much anymore. You'll get the hang of it," she said. "How long are you going to be here?"

"Just for the summer, and then my family goes back home and I go back to school."

"Well, even if it's just for a while it will be good to have somebody close to my age around here."

"How old are you?" I asked.

"I'll be fifteen in two weeks. Perhaps you and your brother can come to a little party my mother's throwing in the cafeteria for my birthday."

"That would be nice. Thank you."

"Well, here's our next stop," Sally said. "The Prop Shop."

That was where Ray worked. I would have liked to say hi, but it had been made very clear to all of us that we couldn't let on we knew him—it could "blow our cover." My mother said she'd be happy if we could just keep it that way.

The Prop Shop was a large, plain-looking building a good distance from the main house. It looked as though it might have been a coach house back when they had horses and carriages at Bletchley. Sally pulled open a large sliding door and we were greeted by a dozen men who looked like they were having a party.

"Come and join our celebration!" one of the men yelled out.

Before we could say yes or no a second fellow pushed glasses of lemonade into our hands.

"Thank you," I said. "What are you celebrating?"

"We just got confirmation that the Germans bombed our airfield!"

"They dumped hundreds of tons of bombs on it," the first man yelled. "Practically blew it off the face of the earth!"

The two men clinked glasses triumphantly.

"I . . . I don't understand," I stammered. Why would that be something to celebrate?

"Here, I'll show you, come, come and see!"

The first man led us through the party to a set of photos pinned to the wall.

"Do you see the destruction, the number of bomb craters, the destroyed planes? The place took such a beating there must have been a whole squadron of German bombers dropping their ordnance on it."

"And you're happy about that?"

"Not just happy, we're ecstatic!"

"You're ecstatic that one of our air bases was destroyed?" Words practically failed me. These people weren't just quiet sympathizers, they were celebrating the destruction of one of our bases. I had to go straight to the commander and have them all arrested and—

"I think you're confusing our young friends."

I knew the voice. I turned around. It was Ray. He gave me a wink that I hoped nobody else noticed.

"Tell them why we're all so happy," Ray said.

"Oh, that's right, it must sound like we've all gone off our rockers!"

"Bonkers!" said another man.

"Stark raving mad!" said a third. "It wasn't a *real* airfield, of course."

I looked at him, then at the pictures pinned to the wall, and then back at him. If I hadn't thought he was crazy before I certainly did now.

"This is all a big illusion," Ray said. "It isn't a real airfield, it's all made up."

"How can an airfield be made up?" Sally asked.

"That tarmac is simply dirt painted black," Ray said, pointing out a detail in one of the pictures.

"And those airplanes that were destroyed on the

ground were canvas and wood. So were the barracks for the men, and the hangars. We spent a great deal of time making it look real."

"And the Germans blew it all sky high!" another man yelled.

A cheer went up and another round of toasts began. I had a feeling that most of these men weren't drinking lemonade.

"But shouldn't you be upset that they destroyed all your hard work?" Sally asked.

I understood now why they were celebrating, but I couldn't really say anything without risking my reputation as a dumb new kid.

"Oh, no, young lady. The greatest compliment the Germans can give us is bombing our handicraft. If they hadn't thought it was real they wouldn't have dropped bombs on it," the man said.

"And because they dropped all those hundreds of bombs here they didn't drop them elsewhere, like on a real airfield," Ray said. "So now can you understand why this is such a cause for celebration?"

"It makes sense," I said.

"If you are in a play and you've done well the audience will give you a standing ovation," one of the men said.

"A fine opera singer will receive calls of 'Bravo!' and requests for an encore."

"A painter will have his art purchased and displayed in a museum," Ray said. "But for the members of the Prop Shop, the dropping of bombs on our work is the highest compliment."

"So let's raise a glass in celebration. Tomorrow we'll put that airfield back together and we'll hope the Germans see fit to destroy it one more time."

They clinked glasses again and continued their celebration.

"We have to deliver this envelope and get on our way," Sally said, holding it out.

"I'll take it," Ray said.

She handed him the big brown envelope, then we turned and left the building and the party behind.

"You were asking about people who are different?" Sally said. "That one who took the envelope, there's something about him that I just don't trust."

"I'll keep that in mind. Thanks for the warning."

Funny, one of the few people at Bletchley who I could trust was the one person she didn't trust.

"We have one more stop before the day is over," Sally said. "We have to deliver this parcel to the bombe room."

"They make bombs here?"

"Oh, gracious no . . . at least, I don't know if they do. It's not 'bomb,' like an explosive, but 'bombe' with an *e* at the end. I think it's French or Polish or something."

That was reassuring. After almost being blown up at the DIL munitions plant in Ajax I hoped to never be close to a bomb again.

"It's a series of big cabinets . . . well, not cabinets, machines . . . I don't know how to explain it, but I can show you. Just don't expect to be able to talk while we're in there, or even hear yourself think."

We went back into the main building, once again weaving down halls, along corridors and through doors. I was starting to think that she was underestimating just how complex this place was. I might not ever be able to find my way around. Once again I was impressed not only with her ability to find her way through the maze but also by the fact that she seemed to know everybody along the route we were walking. This was apparently the perfect job if you wanted to get to know everyone. I had been given the perfect cover.

"Do you hear it?" Sally asked.

I heard something, but I wasn't sure what it was. It sounded sort of like a car running. Sally opened a door and the noise became even louder. We stepped in. There were five large cabinets, and in each was a series of large, copper-coloured wheels spinning around and each seemed to be making a *clickety-clickety* sound. It wasn't really like the sound of a car engine, more like the noise from about a million little toy trains running along the tracks.

Women, and it was all women, were fiddling with the wheels and popping in and out from behind the cabinets, looking like little figures in an arcade shooting game. I had no idea what was happening, but it was eardrum-shatteringly loud.

Sally leaned in close to a woman and they yelled out words that I couldn't hear. Then she handed the woman the big envelope she had been carrying. They nodded, smiled at each other, and then Sally motioned to the exit. I was happy to get outside and close the door behind us. The noise was still echoing in my head.

"That was really, really loud," I said.

"You'd better get used to it. You'll make more deliveries in there than any other room in the whole place."

"Why is that?"

"Each of the huts sends messages there daily, many times, and then messages go back."

"So the other huts don't communicate with each other, but each hut communicates with that room?" I said.

"Exactly."

"And do other parts of the Bletchley compound have communications with each other that way?" I asked.

Sally shook her head. "Most of them work in isolation. Mail comes in and goes out but not between them. Although, really, other than making a lot of noise, I have no idea what goes on in there."

I didn't know exactly what they did in there either but I knew it had to be essential if every single codebreaking hut was connected to that one room. If I'd been an enemy agent and wanted to infiltrate or destroy just one place, that would be it. Planting a bomb in the bombe room would be what I'd try to do.

Knowing *who* the enemy agents were would be the best thing. Knowing *where* they would strike was second best. For my first day on the job, I was happy enough to have second best.

CHAPTER TWELVE

MY FATHER SCOOPED out another big spoonful of beans and plopped them down on my plate. I was hungry, but if this meal was anything like most of the meals he cooked, the beans were going to be half burned and half cold.

"Do you want more?" he asked.

I didn't know if I wanted anything, ever, that he cooked. "No, that's good, thank you."

We took our plates over to the kitchen table and sat down.

"I know I'm not the cook your mother is," he confessed.

Jack smirked but kept his head down.

"I was really hoping that your mother would be able

to make dinner tonight, but she seems too occupied to come home," my father said. "Again."

I knew if I were working on Shark I'd probably still be there as well. She had been working sixteen-hour days all week while the rest of us were doing a regular eight-hour shift every day.

"So, did you learn anything interesting today?" my father asked.

"I learned that the whole place is so old and rundown it might fall down by itself," Jack said. I noticed that he was spending more time pushing his beans around his plate than actually eating them. I guess he missed Mom's cooking too.

"And you, George?"

I'd learned how to find my way around and was starting to get to know people.

"I'm even more positive I've figured out which room is the most important in the whole of Bletchley Park, the place I'd aim for if I wanted to do the most damage."

"The bombe room is the heart of the place," he confirmed.

Sally hadn't been joking. I was continually delivering

messages to and from the bombe room. It was like the hub of a gigantic wheel, and all the spokes from other buildings led right to it.

"And if you knew the place at all it wouldn't be very hard to get in there," my father said. "The security is atrocious . . . not that the head of security believed me when I told him about the obvious problems." My father had become increasingly distressed about this.

"Why won't he listen to you?" Jack asked.

"He's like an ostrich with his head in the sand. I told him that an enemy agent could probably stroll in completely undetected." My father shook his head.

"Why don't they just do the obvious stuff to make it really secure?" Jack said. "Put up higher fences and more guards and add some real tanks and machine-gun nests?"

"I was told that they have to keep security as unobtrusive as possible because they're afraid that more security would attract more attention," my father said.

"I guess that does make some sense," I said. "If you make something appear well defended, people are going to assume there must be something in there worth defending."

"But if you posted enough guards and made the fences high enough it wouldn't matter that people noticed because you could keep them out," Jack argued.

"You can keep people out, but you can't keep bombs out," my father said. He pointed upward. "They're afraid of German bombers."

"You can't defend against that."

"You can if you put up enough anti-aircraft guns and Spitfires," Jack said.

"If that were foolproof then London and all those other cities wouldn't have been blitzed, and the Germans would have given up bombing long ago," my father pointed out.

"But don't they target railroads and railway stations?" Jack asked. "And aren't we right beside the Bletchley Station?"

My father nodded. "You make a good point, the location here is vulnerable. That's probably why they believe that their best defence is for nobody to know what's going on here, so no one thinks of attacking. If the enemy had even a hint of the work being done here, then you can be sure that there wouldn't be enough ack-ack guns in the world to keep it safe."

"Yes, but still, a few more guards, some higher fences and some barbed wire wouldn't be that obvious," my brother said.

"You're preaching to the choir, son. I agree completely. I just wish we could convince the commander of that. He says they have sufficient security in place."

"Well, I guess there's one way to convince him he's wrong," I said.

"And what would that be?" my father asked.

Jack leaned over and put a hand on my shoulder. He was smiling. He knew. "We break in."

"You can't just break in," my father said.

"Why not? We broke into the DIL plant in Ajax," Jack said.

"You did?"

"I guess we never mentioned that," I said.

"The Camp X guys used to break in all the time to test security," Jack explained.

"Although we didn't really break in so much as we

walked in through the front gate. We sort of bluffed our way past the guards," I said.

"That wouldn't work at Bletchley because you're allowed to be here," my father said.

"We wouldn't go in through the gate," Jack said. "We could cut across the forest and through the fence. We can do it."

My father didn't answer right away, which meant he was thinking this through.

"If this is to be any kind of real test, it will have to be done in complete secrecy," he said.

"We're very, *very* good at secret," Jack said.

I nodded enthusiastically.

"I don't just mean keeping it a secret from the commander, or the guards. I'm talking about your mother. If she finds out, there's no way she's going to agree to this . . . although I don't like keeping secrets from her."

"It doesn't have to be a secret," I said. "You can tell her as soon as you see her . . . of course, if we try to break in tonight you won't be seeing her before that."

My father gave me a stern look. "Do you know how

much trouble I'd be in with your mother if I let you two go on your own and break into Bletchley?"

I did have a pretty good idea.

"So, the only way this can happen is if all three of us break in," he said.

I did a double take. Did he really just say that?

My father smiled. "I can't let you two have *all* the fun."

Less than two hours later we were lying on our bellies, dressed in black and with mud smeared on our faces, at the very edge of the forest that stretched out across the back of Bletchley Park. In front of us was an open stretch of grass, beyond which was a fence topped with barbed wire, another patch of grass and then the back door to Bletchley. We had been watching the guards on patrol walking the back of the property, just inside the fence. One had just disappeared in one direction while the other had vanished into the darkness in the other direction.

"Now," my father whispered.

Quietly but quickly we moved across the grass, crouching low, hoping we were invisible. We dropped to our knees at the base of the fence. My father grabbed the wire strands at the bottom and pulled up until they came off the ground just far enough for Jack to slip underneath. I quickly followed, and then Jack and I both grabbed the bottom of the fence and yanked it up for our father. The wire dug into my hands. I was grateful that part of the plan involved us wearing gloves.

"Not much time," my father said. "Quick."

We avoided the gravel path and ran on the grass to silence our steps. We had just made it to the edge of the building when we heard footsteps. We froze, pressed against the building and hopefully hidden in the shadows, as first one sentry and then the other appeared again on their rounds. They walked along the fence, approaching each other, their features becoming clearer as they closed the distance. I could see the details of their uniforms, revolvers strapped to their sides, rifles on their shoulders.

Strange, I had known they had guns, but seeing them sent a little shiver up my spine. If they saw us, would they shoot first and ask questions later? Would we even get a chance to raise our hands and surrender? I couldn't think about that.

The two sentries came closer and closer on either side of us. We could see them so clearly—how could they not see us? I held my breath and closed my eyes. It wasn't because I believed that if I couldn't see them they couldn't see me, it was more because I didn't want them to see the whites of my eyes. The sound of their heavy boots against the gravel got louder and louder, filling my ears . . . and then it got quieter. I opened my eyes and for a split second I couldn't locate them. Then I realized that they had met in the middle and then turned around and were walking away. They hadn't seen us.

My father started moving. Jack was behind him, and I trailed at the rear. We were aiming for a door set back in a recess, hidden from the sentries. We slid along the wall until we came to it and—

"It's locked," my father whispered. "I didn't know they locked them at night. We'll have to find another door."

"Or go through this one," Jack said. He turned to me. "George."

I nodded and dropped to one knee in front of the door.

"What are you doing?" my father asked.

"I'm going to pick the lock." Even in the dim light I

could see the surprise on his face. "It's something Ray taught me how to do in Bermuda."

"He's very good at it," Jack said.

I pulled out my lock pick—it was specially designed to look like a pencil. I placed the tip in the lock and then started to *feel* for the tumblers. I closed my eyes again. I always found it easier that way to focus on the touch, and there was really nothing to see anyway.

"The guards will be back soon," my father whispered. "How long will it—?"

Jack shushed him into silence. "He needs to concentrate."

I did. I couldn't worry about anything around me. I had to let the feel of the pick against the tumblers travel through my fingers and up into my head. It was an old-fashioned lock, nothing complicated, just a gigantic keyhole. Of course it wasn't like I practised picking locks very often . . . *click* . . . it opened. I reached up for the doorknob and opened the door—and then froze as the light from a bulb overhead made everything as bright as day.

My father grabbed me and pushed me through the

door. Jack followed and closed the door behind us with a click. We were inside and, as far as we knew, unseen by the guards.

"Which way?" my father asked.

"Where do you want to go?"

"You said you thought the bombe room would be good. Then I'd also like to go to the security chief's office and Commander Travis's office."

"Those last two are trickier. We'll have to go through the main foyer or the cafeteria to get to them and they'll both be filled with people," I said. "And we're not exactly dressed to go unnoticed."

Being in black with mud smeared on our faces worked well out in the dark, but it was hardly the way to blend in with people on the inside.

"We'll move as fast as we can and get as far as we can before somebody tries to stop us," our father said. "The fact that we've already gotten this far without being detected means something. Lead away."

I took us down the hall and then cut through the first open door, which led us into a passageway. I'd been told

that big old Victorian mansions always had servants' corridors for the household staff to take so that the owners
didn't have to mingle with the help. And here it was—a
passage that not many people at Bletchley even knew
about, that Sally had shown me. We used it to deliver mail
when the main corridors were too crowded. Travelling
through here meant we had a better chance to get to
the bombe room before anybody discovered— A door
opened and a man popped out. He looked at us, did a
double take and skidded to a stop.

"I guess we've been discovered," my father whispered.

"Discovered but not stopped," Jack whispered back,
and then, more loudly, "Excuse me, could you come
here, please?" Jack gestured for the man to approach.

The fellow hesitated for a split second and then
walked toward us. Jack smiled and held out his hand as if
to shake, and the man did the same.

"Bang!" Jack said as he took the man's hand.

"Excuse me?" the man asked, more than a bit startled.

"Bang . . . although technically it would have been a
knife instead of a gun. Much quieter, but you're dead just
the same."

The man now looked confused, and he tried to pull his hand away but Jack held firm.

"I get it," my father said to Jack. He turned to the man. "Don't you think it would have been smarter to walk away, or even run away, when you saw the three of us dressed like this?"

"I didn't really think about it." His confused look suddenly took a turn for scared.

"We're doing an exercise to see if we could break in," I explained.

"Oh, I see," he said, although judging by his expression he really didn't. At least he seemed a little relieved as Jack finally released his hand.

"Could you please do us an official favour," my father asked, "and sort of stay dead . . . don't mention this to anybody until the exercise is over?"

"Certainly, I can do that," he said. "Dead men tell no tales, as they say."

"Thank you," my father said. "We'd better let you get on your way, and we'll get on our way."

"Where are you heading?" the man asked.

"The bombe room," my father said.

"Excellent choice!" he exclaimed. "Good hunting!"

He disappeared down the corridor in the opposite direction.

"Do either of you know him?" my father asked.

We both shook our heads.

"Then he probably doesn't know any of us," my father said. "We could have been enemy agents, and he wouldn't have done a thing."

"Not the best security," Jack said.

"That's for sure," my father said. "Now let's get going, and we'll make a point of *killing* whoever else we meet along the way."

My father looked down at the floor while my mother continued to yell at him—at all of us. She was alternating between angry and hysterical, and whichever one she was I wanted her to be the other. I was trying hard not to make eye contact while still letting her know that I was paying attention.

My brother, father and I had gotten back to the guest cottage just before two in the morning. We were all pretty happy. We'd *destroyed* the bombe room and two huts, gotten to the commander's office and even strolled through the cafeteria—and nobody had stopped us! Most of the people scarcely noticed us, and those who did notice us didn't do anything about it. It was as if there were always so many new people around, and people doing unexpected things, that the three of us, even dressed in black with mud covering our faces, didn't seem that out of place.

We had accomplished what we'd set out to do and that made us very happy—a happiness that ended the second we got in the door. Judging from the way my father was acting I think he would rather have been back in Africa facing Rommel and his Panzer divisions than having my mother angry at him. Actually, angry was okay, it was the tears that were hard.

"Do you have any idea how much you three scared me?" my mother asked again.

"I'm so sorry, dear," my father said. "We are all so sorry."

Jack and I nodded our heads solemnly and enthusiastically, trying to look apologetic.

"I thought you were all kidnapped, or dead or—" She

burst into tears again, and my father tried to comfort her, but she brushed his arms away.

"Not that this is any excuse," my father said, "but we thought we'd be home long before you got back or we never would have—"

"Never would have told me what you did?" she demanded.

"Never would have worried you. I would have told you."

"Told me that you brought our boys along on a fool's mission? You put them—*you*—in danger."

"We've been in situations a lot more dangerous than that," Jack said. "Lot of times, me and George have faced things that—"

She started sobbing even louder. Jack looked even sorrier.

"The important thing is that we're safe," my father said. "And believe me, we won't do that again."

"I can't believe any of you," she said. "It was bad enough when I only had two boys to try to keep out of trouble."

"I'm so sorry, dear."

"You could have gotten yourself and your sons shot! Those guards do carry guns, you know!"

"I was only doing my job, the way you were doing yours," my father said. "By the way, why did you come home before the end of your shift?"

"I received a message," she said. "An important message."

We waited for her to continue, but she didn't seem in any rush.

"I feel so upset . . . I don't even know if I'm going to go," she said.

"Go where?" my father asked.

"Tomorrow, at one o'clock, we have an audience with Louise and her family."

"I'm going to see Louise!" Jack exclaimed.

"A car is being sent around to pick us up."

"In that case," my father said, "maybe we should all go to bed. I have to be up early enough to tell the security chief exactly what happened tonight before we leave."

"Yeah, we'd better get to bed," Jack said. He got to his feet and I did the same.

"You two are *not* going to bed," our mother said. "At least not until you go and wash up. Look at you! Were you wallowing in a pigpen? You are both *filthy*!"

CHAPTER THIRTEEN

MY MOTHER WAS TRYING to give us the silent treatment—still angry about last night—but it wasn't working very well. She was too excited. Maybe the only person more excited was Jack, but he was working very, very hard—and just as unsuccessfully—not to show it. I'd already caught him at the bathroom mirror first thing in the morning fussing with his hair.

Jack and I were dressed in our best brought-from-Bermuda clothes—starched white shirts, jackets and black dress pants, and ties borrowed from our father. My mother had carefully ironed out the wrinkles, made us polish our shoes till they shone, and personally scrubbed the last little bit of mud from behind our ears. She was wearing her pearls with her best "going to church" dress, topped off with white gloves and a hat and her newest handbag. My father had it the easiest. He was wearing his captain's uniform, and he looked pretty sharp. I would have liked to have been in a uniform, too.

Now we were in the car that had been sent for us, with our own driver, and feeling pretty special as we sped along the roadway toward . . . well, they hadn't actually said where we were going, exactly.

"The countryside is very beautiful," my mother said. "It's all so lush and green and peaceful."

"It's hard to believe there's even a war going on," my father said.

"I think that's why members of the royal family stay out here, away from the city," she replied.

"Or send their kids to Canada or Bermuda," Jack added. "I know Louise is just glad to be home with her family."

Louise had returned to England the night after the attempted kidnapping. Obviously the Nazis knew who she was, and where she was, so Bermuda wasn't safe for her anymore. How ironic that she'd been sent from England to Bermuda to get away from danger, and it had followed her all the way across the Atlantic Ocean!

"You two have certainly been keeping the postman busy," my mother said to Jack with a smile.

My mother seemed quite taken by the idea of her son having a "sweetheart." Of course, comments like that only made Jack cringe with embarrassment. As for me, I thought the whole thing was stupid. It wasn't that I didn't like Louise, but what was the point in having a girlfriend who lived so far away, separated by an ocean filled with enemy U-boats? Besides, she was royalty, and Jack, well . . . wasn't. I was only twelve but I was smart enough to know there was no future in this. No future and no present—just a past, and how long would that last?

We'd been in the car for over an hour already and the driver, friendly and open about everything else, had explained that he couldn't tell us where we were going or how long it would take. And with all the signs taken off the roads, we didn't have much of an idea where we were other than in the countryside somewhere. I'd hoped we were going to London, but it seemed as if we were heading even farther into the country.

The car slowed down and made a turn. I gawked and strained my neck to peer out the window. We were driving through lush, well-tended gardens and up ahead was a massive stone building—a castle!

"We have arrived," the driver said.

"Louise lives in a castle!" Jack exclaimed.

"Not *a* castle," the driver said. "*The* castle. This is *Windsor* Castle."

"Windsor is the home of the King!" my mother said.

"One of his homes," the driver said. "Since the war began, many members of the royal family have taken refuge at Windsor."

"I guess it's big enough to hold a whole lot of people," I said.

"At present there are more than eight hundred people who live and work at Windsor."

"It must be huge!" I said.

"The castle itself, excluding the grounds, occupies thirteen acres. It has been continually expanded by successive English monarchs since it was originally established by

William the Conqueror in the eleventh century because of its strategic position on the Thames."

"Is there anything in Canada that old?" I asked my parents.

"I'm sure there are some things that the original people built, but our country is officially only seventy-six years old," my father responded.

"Do you know what they call something seventy-six years old in England?" the driver asked.

"What?" I asked.

"Newly constructed." He laughed. "This is the longest-occupied palace in the world."

"So we might see the King or his family today?" my mother asked.

"You might, but it's not likely. He and his family spend most of their time in London at Buckingham Palace."

"It's an inspiration to have him staying right there to face the bombing," my father said.

"Although it might be better to send his family away to a safer place," my mother added.

"He would have liked that," the driver said. "But I understand the Queen has said that Princess Elizabeth and Princess Margaret wouldn't leave without their mother, and she wouldn't leave without the King, and the King would *never* leave."

"How bad is it in London?" my father asked.

"It's a bit like living on the side of a volcano."

"How's that?" I asked. When I thought of London I didn't exactly think of volcanoes.

"A volcano doesn't have to erupt very often to have you afraid all the time. The bombings are far less frequent, but they still happen more than anybody would like, and with deadly results. Whole sections of the city are nothing but ruins."

"And are people still sleeping in the underground, in the Tube stations?" my mother asked.

"Safest place. Some nights there have been hundreds killed by the bombs."

"Awful, just awful," she said.

"It is. War is terrible enough when it's soldiers killing soldiers, but most of the casualties in London have been civilians, women and children."

"Do you think we'll get to London?" Jack asked.

"It sounds as though it's far too dangerous," my mother said.

"During the day it's not dangerous," the driver said. "The bombers only come at night."

"So we could go during the day?" I asked.

"It would seem wrong to come all this way and not see London," Jack agreed.

"Well . . . we'll see," my father said.

My mother didn't look happy but she didn't argue.

The car pulled up to a large door at the front of the castle. "Here we are. Welcome to Berkshire . . . and to Windsor Castle."

I sat very silently, trying not to spill my tea or get scone crumbs on my clean shirt as the adults made polite conversation. We were all sitting together in a very formal and fairly chilly room with big windows. I guess it seemed formal because everything was so clean and tidy. And there were no personal touches, no knick-knacks or photos in frames, just vases of flowers and a very grand silver teapot that looked as if it might weigh about fifty pounds. Fortunately I didn't have to pick it up because a servant had carried it in on a tray and poured for us.

Louise's parents sat in armchairs on one side of the room, my parents were across from them, and I sat across from Louise and Jack, who shared a small settee. I wasn't really following much of the conversation—too much talk about too little that interested me.

When we'd met Louise's parents, my mother had tried to curtsey and Louise's mother had stopped her and insisted that they all call each other by their first names. She thought being the "Duke" and "Duchess" was rather stuffy. She and her husband seemed nice enough—friendly, and interested in hearing about our home in Canada and what we thought about Bermuda.

Jack wasn't talking much. He was sort of trying to stare at Louise without being obvious about it. If he'd been smart he would have sat where I was sitting. Side by side didn't mean much, because it wasn't like they were going to hold hands or anything—at least I hoped Jack was smart enough to realize that.

"We are so pleased to hear that your stay in England has been extended," Louise's mother said.

"Yes, we could be here for at least two months," my mother replied.

"I hope that means I can see you more than just this one time," Jack said shyly to Louise.

Louise gave him a big smile. I'd kind of forgotten how pretty she was. Maybe I shouldn't have been so quick to tease him about liking her!

"Perhaps another meeting or two can be arranged," her father said. "We all have commitments so it might be difficult. Windsor is not that easy to get to without a driver."

"But London is," Louise said. "I'm often in London, and Bletchley is just a train ride away."

Her father turned to mine. "Yes, I'd been told that you work at Bletchley," he said. "I've heard there are some interesting goings-on up there. What exactly is your assignment?"

"We can't tell you that," I said.

My mother looked shocked. "George, where are your manners?"

"Sorry," I said. I turned back to Louise's father. "We can't tell you, *sir*."

He burst into laughter. "I should have known better than to ask. We can't even tell our daughter what *we* do. I suppose during wartime many of us are called upon to play important roles that will never be widely known."

"Although, as a mother, I can't imagine anything more important than the role you played in saving the life of our daughter," Louise's mother broke in.

"We just did what we had to do," Jack said, glancing sideways at Louise and blushing a bit. "We couldn't stand back and let those stinky Nazis harm your daughter."

I thought, *Stinky. . . is that the word to use?* It made them sound more like bad cheese than evil killers.

"You are both very brave young men," Louise's father said. "And George, you've recovered completely from being shot?"

"I wasn't really shot," I said. " More like grazed by a bullet. It went right by my head, right here."

I showed them the scar, though you could barely see it since most of the hair had grown back. It didn't really bother me at all, although for the first month or so it had been sore and itchy.

"Still, just to have a gun aimed at you, it must have been terrifying," Louise's mother said.

"It all happened so fast I really didn't notice. It was all just a flash, a blur, and then I woke up in the hospital."

"Having had the adventure of a lifetime," her father added.

"Not really. I don't think that was even the scariest thing that's happened . . ." I let the sentence trail off. I couldn't tell him anything else without violating the Official Secrets Act.

"Our son—our *sons*—have had the misfortune to have been involved in many incidents," our mother said, "and the good fortune to have survived them all."

"We will try not to ask any more questions you can't answer," he said. Then he turned again to our father. "I can see by your medals and ribbons that you, sir, were stationed in North Africa."

"Almost two years."

"You know, if you don't mind my saying, I rather envy you. I attempted to enlist for overseas combat myself," Louise's father said, "but it was not allowed. Instead, I have a position here. Actually, my assignment has involved some dealings with Bletchley Park. Perhaps if I'm up there again we could share another cup of tea."

"That would be lovely," my mother said. "In fact, you are all welcome if you'd like to come up. They've given us a very nice cottage to live in."

"A Sunday trip to Bletchley would be charming," Louise's mother said. "We will try to arrange it."

There was another trip I had in mind just then. I felt a little embarrassed to ask, but I had to. I'd had three cups of tea, and what went in had to come out.

"Excuse me," I said. "Do you think I could use the . . . the loo?"

"Of course, my apologies for not explaining earlier," Louise's father said. "The closest facilities are through those doors, down the corridor to the end, then a right and a left, and the door is on the left."

"Do you want us to ring for a servant to escort you?" Louise's mother asked.

"No, I'll be fine," I said. "I'm good with directions."

I got up and headed for the door. They continued to talk and I was grateful to slip out. They did seem like nice people, but still they were a duke and a duchess, and being around them did make me nervous.

The hall was long and wide, lined on both sides with old paintings. I didn't know much about art, but I figured they had to be very valuable. I finally came to the end of the hall and then hung a right into another long hall. This one had paintings too but also suits of not-so-shining armour, with swords and shields, all along one side. In a strange fit of paranoia I wondered if they were empty. Jack was right, I *was* seeing trouble behind every potted plant, and now even inside empty armour.

Carefully I went up to one of the suits. I was amazed at how small it was—this knight would have been shorter than me. I peered into the eyeholes of the face piece and all I could see was darkness. I tapped on the chest plate and it echoed back a hollow sound. Empty. Good.

I came to the end of the hall—did he say go left or right? Both directions led off into the distance. Left, it was left after the right. I walked down the hall trying to be as quiet as possible, but my footsteps still echoed off the walls. This was an incredible house . . . castle. I couldn't imagine living in a place like this. It was more like a museum than a home.

Now I just had to find the actual toilet. I jiggled the handle of the first door. It was locked. So were the second and the third doors, and—

"Can . . . can I help you, young m-m-man?"

I spun around to see a man wearing riding clothing. Was he a riding instructor, or a groom?

"I was looking for the toilet, for the loo, sir."

"Come." He gestured for me to follow.

"Thanks for your help. This place is huge, so I guess I'm a little lost."

"It is easy to g-get lost at first. If you d-don't mind my asking . . . wh-why are you here?"

"My family was invited by Louise's family."

"Ah . . . Louise . . . you are her fr-friend?"

"More my brother. We're having tea together in a big room with windows overlooking the garden."

"Louise is a lovely girl . . . she's a relative of mine."

A relative? That meant he had to be royalty too.

"This is it," he said, stopping at a door.

"Thank you so much, sir."

"You are w-w-welcome. Please say hello for me to Louise and her p-p-parents, and your family."

"Who should I say hello from?"

"Just t-tell them hello from B-Bertie."

"I will. Thanks again for your help."

He smiled as he went his own way and I went into the washroom. He seemed like a very nice man, just like Louise's parents. Maybe all royal people were nice.

Finding my way back was easier—I just retraced my steps past the suits of armour, the paintings, and then through the big doors and back into the sitting room. Everyone else was talking and laughing, but it looked as though I hadn't missed much except a lot more polite small talk.

"Did you find it?" my mother asked.

"I had some help. A man showed me. He asked me to say hello to you . . . he said he's one of Louise's relatives."

"Well, a good many people here at the castle are our relatives. Did he give you his name?" Louise's father asked.

"Yes. He said his name was Bertie."

Louise's father seemed a bit startled. "Oh! I didn't realize he was here today," he said.

"I would have thought he'd be in London," her mother said.

"Do you think Elizabeth and Margaret are here as well?" Louise asked.

"Most likely," her mother said. "I wouldn't imagine he'd leave them at Buckingham Palace without him."

"Buckingham Palace?" my mother asked.

"Yes, that is his official residence," Louise's mother answered.

"Perhaps we should explain. Bertie is the name the family calls him. You probably know him by a more formal title." Louise's father paused. "George, you share a name with the gentleman who helped you find your way . . . Bertie is King George."

"The King of England!" my mother exclaimed. "You met the King of England, George!"

"And you asked him to help you find the washroom!" Jack said with a chuckle.

"I'm so sorry," my mother said. "Please offer our apologies to the King."

"No need to be sorry, or to apologize," Louise's father said. "Bertie is one of the sweetest men you could ever meet."

"Especially where children are concerned," Louise's mother said. "He simply dotes on the princesses. He's very proud of them."

"My son has a real sense of timing," my father said. "He's the only person I know who can go to the loo and end up meeting the King of England."

I wanted to say something about how that was better than the spies, thieves, traitors and murderers I'd been running into lately, but I just smiled and nodded my head.

"So, as we were saying earlier," Louise's mother said, "we will expect to see you in London sometime in the coming weeks."

"Sooner would be even better," Louise said, with a fond glance at Jack.

"I'm just not sure, given all our commitments, that we can expect to get away any time soon," my mother explained.

"Then maybe I could just go to London on my own," Jack suggested.

"And I could meet you," Louise quickly added.

"I don't think that would be appropriate," Louise's father said.

"And besides, Jack, I don't think your going anywhere alone would be wise," my father said.

"I could go with him," I offered.

Jack didn't look too pleased about my suggestion.

"I'm not sure the two of you together guarantees anything short of double the trouble," my mother said.

Jack and Louise both looked disappointed.

"I'm afraid the most we can offer is to do our best to make sure that Jack and Louise see each other during your stay," her father said.

I didn't really care much about seeing Louise—it wasn't like she was my girlfriend—but I sure did want to get to London. To come all the way to England and not see London, to have seen the bombing in newsreels at the movies and not be able to see it in person . . . well . . . that was just plain wrong. I was not going to let that happen.

CHAPTER FOURTEEN

IT WAS TIME FOR LUNCH, and I'd made all my deliveries for the morning. I looked around the dining hall for my mother. She had been working such long days all week that, other than when I made deliveries to Hut 8 or shared a meal with her in the dining hall, I'd hardly seen her at all. She and all the other code breakers were working around the clock, hardly pausing even to eat. She said they were "getting closer," but she was just getting farther from us. In fact, she wasn't in the dining hall today.

I could understand why they were working so hard, and why they were feeling frustrated: they all knew that real lives were at stake. Each day that the Enigma machine remained a mystery, each day that the Shark code remained untamed, meant more ships were in jeopardy and more lives lost. Strange to think that the lives of hundreds, maybe even thousands, of sailors that we'd never see and never know were in the hands of the people in Hut 8. I know the pressure was growing each day. I could see it in my mother's eyes and in the strained look on her face.

My father had also been pretty busy lately—I didn't see him at any of the tables. Since we had "broken into" Bletchley they had agreed to a number of security changes. Fences were being dug into the ground, more sentries had been posted, and some of the doors weren't just being locked but chained up from the inside at night. My father was in charge of all that, and he was taking it just as seriously as my mother was taking her work.

Jack was occupied with minor repairs around the place, but since most of his thoughts were focused on seeing Louise he wasn't much fun to be around even when he was around. He and Louise had spoken on the phone a couple of times—the calls were short and static-filled, with him yelling out what he was trying to say and continually asking, "What did you say?"

With all of them occupied, only one of us was spending any time trying to figure out if anything suspicious was going on around Bletchley. The problem, of course, was that almost everything happening around here was at least little suspicious, or at least peculiar—just like so many of the people.

While I didn't see any of my family in the dining hall, I did recognize a whole lot of people from my rounds, including Ray. He saw me as well and gave me a subtle nod of the head. I would have liked to have sat with him, but we were still pretending not to know each other except from the times I made deliveries to the Prop Shop. If he'd been sitting alone I would have gone over, but there was another man with him at his table and— Ray motioned for me to come over.

"Hello, young man . . . it's George, right?"

"Yes, sir."

"I don't know if you remember me. I'm Ray. And this is my colleague Ian."

"You work in the Prop Shop, right?" I asked. He wasn't the only one who could act.

"Yes, I do, although Ian works in London. He's come up

from the city for a visit. Could you do me a favour, son? We're looking for an outside opinion about something."

"I don't think this is such a wise idea," Ian said.

"Why not?" Ray asked. "He has sworn an oath under the Official Secrets Act. Right?"

"Yes, I have."

"So, showing him the photographs will not compromise security," Ray said. "It isn't like he's a Nazi spy." He paused and looked at me intensely. "You aren't a Nazi spy, are you?" he asked me.

"I'm not a Nazi spy, I promise." Maybe that was the way to find spies at Bletchley—just bring it up in casual conversation and hope they admit it. It wasn't as though my other strategies were getting me anywhere.

"Show him the photos, go ahead," Ray said.

Ian opened up a folder, pulled out a photograph and slid it across the table to me.

"What do you think?" Ray asked.

"Umm . . . it's a picture of some tents taken from up high."

"Taken by aerial reconnaissance," Ian said.

"So what do you think about them?" Ray asked.

I wasn't sure what to say. "They're tents." I shrugged.

"Of course they're tents, but do you know what's inside them?" Ray asked.

"Cots . . . soldiers?" I suggested.

"There are tanks inside those tents," Ray said.

"Real tanks?"

Ray laughed. "We wouldn't hide fake tanks! We only hide real tanks, so the enemy reconnaissance planes won't know they're there."

"That's really smart," I said.

"It *was* smart," Ian said. "At least, the first few times we used that ploy. Now the Nazi intelligence people know we're hiding tanks in tents. The tents don't fool them any longer."

"I still think it will work some of the time," Ray said. "We've shipped so many of those tents to Africa it would be a shame not to use them."

"It's not like they're going to fool anybody," Ian said.

"They fooled the boy," Ray argued.

"He's a boy . . . no offence," Ian said, turning to me.

"None taken."

"I'm just saying that this trick will not fool Nazi intelligence again," Ian said.

"It could," I said. "I guess . . . well, if you . . . I shouldn't say anything . . . it's probably not that good an idea." It was also not a good idea for me to come up with ideas. Looking young and dumb was part of my cover.

"What do you have in mind?" Ray asked.

"Nothing, it was stupid," I mumbled.

"Come on, spit it out, there are no stupid ideas," Ray said.

"Yes, please," Ian said. "I'd like to hear what you have to say."

"Well, I was just thinking that sometimes a magician does things so you can't see what's there, right?" I said.

"Like hiding the tanks in the tents," Ray said.

"Yes. But don't magicians sometimes do things so you think something *is* there that *isn't*?"

"Of course, that's all part of the game," Ray said.

"Well, if the Nazis know that you use those tents to hide tanks in, what if you did the opposite? You put up the tents but there's nothing in them, so the enemy thinks you're hiding tanks when you're not."

Ian and Ray looked at me and then at each other.

"That's interesting. So, rather than using the shell to hide the tanks, you use the empty shell to make them think there are tanks there when there aren't," Ian said.

"You could even have a real tank or two going around and making lots of tracks. They could throw up lots of dust in the wind," Ray said.

"Maybe even put a few dummy tanks in the tents and leave the flaps open so that the aerial photographs catch a few glimpses of what look like real tanks," Ian added.

"That could work, that could really work," Ray said again.

"And then, if they do figure out that you've been using empty tents and so they leave them alone, you can start filling the tents with real tanks again," I said.

"Perfect. The boy has a plan," Ray said. "Not bad for the delivery boy here at Bletchley."

Ian looked at me—closely—as though he was studying me. "So, is that what you're doing here?"

"Um, yeah, delivering letters, envelopes."

"I see," Ian said. "I'm curious, how long have you two known each other?"

"Well, a few weeks, I guess," Ray said. "That's how long you've been here, isn't it?"

"About that. A little longer."

"And you two didn't run into each other in Bermuda?" Ian asked.

"Bermuda?" I asked. I didn't like where this was going.

"Yes, the beautiful island where you lived with your family prior to coming here. The place where your mother worked at the Princess Hotel, which is also where Ray was stationed."

"It's a big island," Ray said. "Thousands of people worked there."

"It's actually a fairly small island," Ian said. "And George would stand out there, the way he did at Camp X."

Camp X! What did he know about me and Camp X?

"I imagine the next thing you're going to tell me is that you've never been to Camp X."

"I don't even know what that is," Ray protested.

"I wasn't talking to you." He turned to face me directly. "I was talking to George."

"What's a Camp X?" I asked, working hard to control my expression and the timbre of my voice.

Ian quietly clapped his hands together. "Very impressive. You are a very convincing liar."

"I don't know what you mean," I said. "I'm not lying about anything."

"Of course you are, and you're doing it very well. In fact, you might have had me doubting myself, if not for the fact that I actually saw you at Camp X on a number of occasions."

Had he really seen me before, or was this just a lie to get me to reveal more than I wanted to?

"George, I wouldn't expect you to remember me. There were so many agents-in-training in and out all the time. But you and your brother certainly stood out. There weren't that many children hanging around the farm."

I took a closer look at him. He did look a little familiar, but . . .

"And even if I didn't remember you, George, I certainly know about your exploits."

He obviously knew some things, but was he pretending to know more so that I would trust him and give him information? Was this some sort of test? Either way, I wasn't going to fall for it.

"Of course, there was nobody at Camp X who didn't know about the role you and your brother played in foiling the attack."

If he'd been stationed at the camp at that time he would certainly have known all about that, so he was telling the truth—at least about seeing me there.

"I also heard what happened afterward at Camp 30, and that is even more remarkable," Ian said. "Practically falling into that tunnel and being kidnapped and almost forced onto a German U-boat—that must have been terrifying."

More than I was going to show or acknowledge. Okay, he did know a lot.

"Then I was briefed about the attempt to destroy the DIL munitions plant, and how you and your brother almost single-handedly saved it from sabotage. Rather remarkable."

Was there anything he *didn't* know?

"George, my clearance is above Top Secret," Ian said.

"He's not fooling with that," Ray said. "I should have known better than to try to put one past him."

"Are you a code breaker?" I asked.

"Oh, no, those people are geniuses," Ian said.

"It takes a bit of a genius to do what you do," Ray said.

"You're being too generous, my friend. I simply play with words and ideas." He turned to me. "Prior to the war I dabbled in writing, and I am now employed in Naval Intelligence, devising ploys and scenarios to fool the enemy."

"I don't know what that means," I said.

Ian laughed. "Still playing the innocent . . . good for you, lad."

"I'm not playing. I don't know."

"Georgie, just think of him as a fancy magician who uses words to try to trick his audience, who happen to be the enemy," Ray said.

"So you come up with things like the tents to hide the tanks?" I asked.

"That idea was conceived by our good friend Victor, but certainly we trade in ideas. As Sun Tzu said twenty-four hundred years ago, 'All of warfare is based on deception.'"

"Like faking airfields to get them to attack the wrong place," I said.

"Exactly. Apparently you're not just delivering mail but gathering information," he said.

I didn't answer. I wasn't going to let him trick me into telling him things just because he was telling *me* things.

"Ultimately, the goal is to come up with something as brilliant as the Haversack Ruse," Ian said.

"I don't know if even I know that one," Ray said.

"Since it happened over thirty years ago I don't think I'm giving away any secrets. It is a good story, and I love a good story," Ian said.

"I know you do," Ray said. "I imagine that someday, long after this war is over, you're going to be making your living as a writer."

"That would be a fine career."

"I just figure that someday I'll be walking into a book-store and asking the clerk for a copy of the newest mys-tery book by that bestselling author *Ian Fleming*."

"From your mouth to God's ear," Ian said. "Now back to *this* story, which was conceived by Field Marshal Edmund Allenby. It was the First World War—the Great War—and we were battling against combined German and Turkish forces in Palestine. We were outnumbered and outgunned."

"That sounds familiar," Ray said.

"But we weren't outsmarted. Allenby created plans for an attack and sent them by courier. His courier was attacked by a German patrol, and while he escaped, he *accidentally* dropped his haversack, in which he'd been carrying the plans for the attack."

"I would imagine that 'accidentally' was rather deliberate," Ray said.

Ian smiled. "*Losing* the plans was a major *part* of the plan. The plans were for a fake attack. The Germans were so pleased with their intelligence coup that they pulled out their forces from one area to defend against the fake attack, weakening their defences. The real attack came against those weakened positions, so of course our forces overwhelmed the enemy and won the real battle."

"That is brilliant!" Ray exclaimed.

"I just wish we could come up with something that brilliant again. An ultimate invasion of Europe is going to need its own Haversack Ruse."

"What if you just did the same thing again?" I asked.

"Unfortunately, the Germans know the story too," Ian said. "They won't be fooled by another haversack."

"He's right," Ray said. "A good magician can't keep performing a trick once the audience is on to it; it doesn't fool anybody. Ian, do you have any new ideas?"

"Even if I had one, you know there are some things that I simply could not talk about to anybody. But really, not yet, still thinking. Do either of you have an idea?"

"Me?" I asked.

"Why not you? Little Bill once told me you were the best twelve-year-old spy in the world," Ian said. He knew Little Bill—that explained so much. "As you well know, Little Bill is quite a remarkable man," Ian continued. "If ever I do get around to writing my novel, a good spy story, I'm sure there will be more than a little of him in there."

I could see Little Bill being a character in a spy book because, really, he seemed more like a made-up character than a real person.

"About the only thing Ian likes more than a good story is a good gadget," Ray said. "Do you have anything interesting on you right now?"

Ian smiled. He reached into his pocket and pulled out a pen. He handed it to Ray.

"What do you think this is?" Ian asked.

"I'm assuming it's not a pen," Ray said.

Ian took it back. "Wrong. It is a pen." He scribbled on the edge of one of the pictures. "But it's more than just a pen. Do you know how they say that the pen is mightier than the sword?"

"I've heard that expression. Still, I think it's better to bring a sword than a pen to a fight," Ray said.

"And even better to bring a gun." Ian pulled up a little clip on the side of the pen. "This is the trigger, and this is a gun."

"A gun!" Ray exclaimed.

"One shot, one bullet."

"And it really works?"

"It's deadly from close range—anything inside two or three feet—but you only get the one shot, so you have to make it count."

"Can I see it?" Ray asked.

Ian folded down the little clip. "You can not only see it, you can have it."

"Thank you so much!"

"I have another one back at the office. Besides, I think you're the only person in the world who appreciates a good gadget even more than I do. Just don't go shooting yourself, or anybody else on our side."

"I'll be careful."

"Now, there is only one question that remains unanswered," Ian said. "What exactly are you doing here, George?"

I wouldn't have cared if it was the King of England asking me that question—I wasn't going to tell him anything.

"I deliver mail and packages," I said.

He smiled. "George, if you were simply delivering mail there would be no need for you and Ray to pretend you have no prior knowledge of each other. My best guess is that you are here to test security measures, or perhaps to report on suspicious behaviour."

I shrugged.

"You do have the perfect cover. Who would suspect a twelve-year-old of doing anything except delivering mail?" Ian said. "Especially one who has such an innocent look and an ability to lie with such a straight face."

"He does have the look of a choirboy about him," Ray said.

"Have you given any thought to bringing him with you on your trips to London?" Ian asked.

"I hadn't," Ray said. "At least, not until now. He would be perfect."

"You could approach practically anybody and they would talk to you."

"Could you two tell me what you're talking about?" I asked. I was feeling anxious.

Ray shook his head. "I can't tell you anything, at least not yet. I have to go and speak to Edward first to see if he'll give me permission."

Before I could say another word Ray jumped to his feet and practically ran off.

"I think you're about to add another interesting chapter to your life story," Ian said.

I swallowed hard. Interesting was such an *interesting* word—it could mean almost anything, from awesome adventure to deadly disaster!

CHAPTER FIFTEEN

I SAT QUIETLY in a chair as Commander Travis continued his telephone conversation. He was speaking on a green phone, which meant that it was a secure line and the conversation was important and confidential. And because he'd been on the phone when his secretary shepherded me into the room, I also assumed that the call might be about me. While I listened to the one-sided conversation I couldn't help but stare at the wallpaper in his office, which featured Peter Rabbit and his friends. Apparently this had been a child's bedroom at one point before it became the commander's office.

"Yes, of course," Commander Travis said. "Thank you

for your candour . . . yes . . . I will pass that on. Thank you for your time."

He put down the phone. "Little Bill sends his regards."

"That was Little Bill?"

"I needed to speak to him about what Ray suggested. While the decision was not his to make, since it involves you I felt I ought to consult him."

All afternoon I'd been delivering the mail, but my mind had been busy reaching for possibilities. What, exactly, did Ray have in mind for me? Now it looked as though I was about to find out.

"I know that you and Ray have a shared history in Bermuda, but I need to make sure that you know the rest of his rather . . . unique history."

"Little Bill told me some things, and so did Ray. I know he was in jail when the war started."

"Yes, he was, as we say, a 'guest of the King.' But it was determined that his special talents could be best utilized in the defence of our nation, in our war efforts. And, I must say, he has been of exceptional use."

"I've seen him in operation in Bermuda as well as here," I said.

"Yes, you have seen some of his work here, in the Prop Shop. But he has another role, as a recruiter. Let me explain. As you know, we need the best minds working on our code-breaking teams. We draw many of our people from predictable sources—they're math professors, scientists, and of course people whose talents are known to us personally. But we also look further afield. We have found that many of our best code breakers are simply people who are able to very quickly do crossword puzzles or play chess or—"

"Or play word games well," I added. "Like my mother."

"Your mother was a *very* good find," he said. "Not only does she have the kind of mind necessary to break codes, but she speaks German. Do you know how valuable those two skills combined are?"

"I guess a lot."

"It's not only very valuable but very rare. She is making such an important contribution."

I felt proud—and for some reason uneasy.

"Ray seems to have a knack for finding potential code breakers in unusual places, striking up a conversation and bringing them to Bletchley to be interviewed. He has been responsible for finding many talents. What would you think about going along with him on one of his little hunts?"

"Hunts?"

"It does sound rather dramatic. You would accompany him to London and frequent some places where these potential code breakers might be."

"What sorts of places?" I asked, although going to any-place in London was fine with me.

"Libraries, chess club meetings, university lounges. Nothing too exciting, I'm afraid."

"But they're in London . . . I'd get to go to London."

"Yes, in London."

"Do you think my brother could come along?" I knew how much he wanted to go down there—especially if Louise was going to be in town.

"Actually, that has already been agreed to," Commander Travis said. "In fact, your father was rather insistent that Jack go along with you, assuming Little Bill was not opposed to either of you being involved."

"And has my mother agreed to us going as well?" I asked. "With Ray?"

"She was a little more reluctant. She is understandably a bit mistrustful of Ray, but I assured her that he has proven himself a man of integrity, and that I would trust him with my life, or the lives of *my* children. Ultimately she felt that it was in the best interests of *everybody*, so she agreed."

Was I imagining it, or had he put extra emphasis on the word "everybody"? Did it have a special meaning? I thought about asking, but what was the point? Nobody ever gave away more than they had to around here.

"You and Jack will be accompanying Ray on his trip tomorrow."

"Can you just hurry up?" Jack asked as we walked out the door of our cottage.

"We're not going to be late. And even if we are, Ray will wait—the next train is only thirty minutes later."

"I don't want to catch the next train. I want to catch this one. It's important."

If the fact that Jack smelled of aftershave wasn't a big enough tipoff, his insistence on catching this specific train practically yelled out that he was up to something, and I had a pretty good idea what it was.

"Is she meeting us at the station in London or is she already on the train?" I asked.

"Who?"

"Please, don't pretend to be stupid . . . although with you maybe it isn't so much pretending as—"

Jack grabbed my arm and spun me around. "How would you like me to wipe that smug look off your face?"

"You could try, and you could probably do it, but I'm pretty sure we'd miss the train."

He let go of my arm. "Louise is on the train."

"Now, wasn't that easy? Look, I don't care if she's on the train or not."

"You'd better not care . . . or say anything. I may not have time now to knock the stuffing out of you but there will be a time and a place."

"Do her parents know about her meeting up with you today?"

"No, they think she's off to spend the day with one of her school friends. Which, if you think about it, isn't really a lie, because I am one of her friends from school . . . in Bermuda."

"They say that the best lie always has some truth at its

core," I said. "I'm just surprised her parents let her travel on her own."

"She told me that she'd be escorted right to the train and put aboard. Besides, they think she's only going one stop along the line, not down to London."

"Smart plan, unless somebody gives it away."

"Are you threatening to tell?" Jack asked.

"I was thinking more of Mom or Dad spilling the beans the next time we meet with Louise's parents."

"And that's why you're not going to tell them," Jack threatened.

"Not me, but what about Ray? He knows Louise, and he knows who she is."

"I'll ask him to keep quiet. Or maybe it would be better if you asked him. Would you?"

"You've asked so nicely, how can I say no?"

"Thank you," Jack said.

"I only ask that next time you think about how much more effective it is to ask me nicely instead of threatening to knock the stuffing out of me."

Jack gave me a tight smile, but he didn't dare say another word in case I changed my mind.

We walked through the gates of Bletchley Park and toward the station. Despite the early-morning hour the streets were busy—shift change was going to be happening soon. As we approached the station, the platform was already starting to fill up.

"Do you see Ray?" Jack asked.

I looked up and down the platform. I couldn't see him.

"No point in us being here on time if Ray doesn't show up," Jack said. "But whether he's here or not, I'm getting on the train with Louise."

"You can't do that. We can't go down to London without Ray."

"Well, I'm not letting Louise go down on her own. You can wait for him and meet us at Victoria Station."

"Mom would kill you if she found out you went down without me. I'm sure he's going to be here and . . . wait . . . Ray might already be here."

Jack gave me a questioning look.

"He could be in disguise."

"Yeah, that would be like Ray. So . . . which one do you think he is?"

We both scanned the crowd on the platform, but everybody looked pretty normal.

I shook my head. "He could be dressed as anything—an old man, a general, or even a priest."

"Oh great, that narrows it down. Come on."

Slowly we walked up the platform, looking closely at people but trying not to be too obvious about it. Nearly half of the people were in uniform, and two-thirds were women. That should have made it easier, but I knew Ray had dressed like a woman before, and he was small enough to not stand out. That was, in fact, probably the best way to tell if it was Ray—he could change a lot of things, but he couldn't make himself taller. We could bypass anybody who was taller than Jack.

"The train will be here soon," Jack said. "What do we do if we can't find him?"

"What if you got on the train, found Louise and brought her to the platform to wait with us here?"

"That could work, but let's keep looking."

We continued up the platform, eliminating potential candidates, but more people were appearing as the time for the train's arrival got closer. We passed by a man sitting on a bench, his face blocked by the newspaper he was reading. I slowed down and then came to a stop. I had the feeling that the man was turning the paper to follow us as we passed. Ray had told me once about using newspapers with tiny holes so you could look through them and watch what was going on without anybody noticing. Could that be Ray, behind that newspaper? There was only one way to be sure.

"Excuse me, sir," I said.

Slowly the newspaper was lowered and Ray smiled up at me. "Good morning, gentlemen." He spoke with a very formal accent and was dressed like a very proper English gentleman, in a tidy three-piece suit and a bowler hat.

"Nice duds," Jack said with a grin.

"I am in the disguise of a dignified member of the upper class . . . perhaps somebody who was educated in one of our finest schools. I was wondering, what exactly gave me away this time, if you don't mind telling me?"

"The newspaper," I said.

"You recognized me from the newspaper?"

"No, it's just that I *didn't* recognize anybody else so I

thought about the newspaper being like a tent hiding a tank, and there you were," I explained.

Just then we heard the train coming.

"We need to go to the last car," Jack said.

"We're meeting somebody," I explained.

Ray looked a little surprised.

"Louise," Jack said, jumping in quickly. "I hope that's okay."

"It might actually help," Ray said. "Here I am trying to pretend to be aristocratic, and you're bringing along royalty."

The train steamed into the station, all smoke and thunder, pushing a rush of warm air in front of it. When it came to a stop people surged forward toward the doors of the cars. We walked along the platform until we reached the final car and climbed on board, Jack in the lead.

Off a narrow corridor there were several small compartments, each with room for four passengers in facing seats. The corridor was crowded with people looking for empty compartments. Luckily, Louise poked her head out her door and waved for us. When Jack pushed his way through the crowd to her compartment, Louise threw her arms around him and they kissed. I couldn't imagine why anybody would want to kiss Jack.

"Nothing more touching than young love," Ray said. "Let's find another compartment and give them some privacy."

That was fine with me—better than fine. Until I saw them kiss I'd forgotten how goofy they could get, and how uncomfortable it could get around them.

We found an empty compartment at the end of the car. Ray sat down in a seat by the window and I took the seat opposite him as the train bumped forward slightly. We were on our way.

"I was pleased that your mother allowed you and Jack to come along today," Ray said. He was now speaking in his regular voice instead of that upper-crust accent. There was no one there to notice.

"I'm glad too."

"I know she doesn't trust me," Ray said. "Not that I can blame her. If I had children I don't think I'd be wanting them hanging out with no jailbird."

"I'm sure she doesn't think of you that way," I said. That was probably a lie.

"Well, you know it's true. Before all of this came up I was in jail, a career criminal."

"You're different now."

"I am different. I'm trying my best to make up for what I did wrong by doing things right."

"Little Bill told me what a big contribution you've made."

"That's quite the compliment, especially coming from him. He's a good man, a decent man," Ray said. "Still, I wish your mother could see I'm trying, too."

"Well, we're allowed to be here with you today—I guess that says something," I pointed out.

"Yes, I guess so . . . So, how are things coming with Shark?" Ray asked.

"She doesn't talk about it."

"Not at all?"

I shook my head.

"And even if she did you wouldn't tell me, would you?" Ray asked.

"You know I couldn't."

"Quite right. I guess it's just idle curiosity on my part. While I'm playing with canvas and wood at the Prop

Shop the whole future of the war is being determined in those huts. Enigma is everything. Can you blame me for wondering?"

"Not at all."

"It's all going on right there beside us and we don't know," Ray said. "I hate not knowing. At least you go in there to deliver the mail. You probably know more than I do."

I was becoming increasingly uncomfortable and wanted to change the subject. "So what exactly is going to happen today?"

"Actually, it's already started happening." He leaned closer. "I noticed a fellow on the train platform doing a crossword puzzle. He's in the compartment behind ours now. Go have a look."

I got up and pulled the door open to exit our compartment, then walked slowly along the corridor until I could see into the next one. Trying not to stare, I took note of a somewhat overweight and red-faced older gentleman holding a pen in one hand and a newspaper in another, with a look of intense concentration. People who were good at crossword puzzles could become code breakers, I knew. Was this a potential recruit for Bletchley?

"I saw him," I told Ray when I got back to our compartment.

"Is he still working on that puzzle?" he asked me.

"Yes. Are you going to talk to him?"

Ray shook his head.

"Do you want me to talk to him?" I asked.

"Oh, goodness no. He's been working on that same puzzle all morning, and he's hardly gotten a word. He's bloody terrible!"

I laughed. "Okay, but how do we find people who aren't terrible? Do we just keep riding around until we see somebody with a completed crossword puzzle?"

"Sometimes we do find them that way, even just riding the Tube, but today we're going to be a little more, shall we say, scientific. We'll be in London by nine, and we're going to one chess tournament in the morning and then another in the afternoon."

"I guess we're lucky that both of those are happening today," I said.

"Luck had nothing to do with it. Both events were

organized by Bletchley staff to provide a place where we
might recruit some new code breakers."

"That's really good thinking."

"It is, if I do say so myself. We'll watch the tournaments
unfold, and see if anybody there is worth approaching."

"And if so, do you just go up and ask them?"

"I go up and start an innocent discussion. That's where
you come in, my dear *nephew*. We'll strike up a conversation and then look for more potential, see if they're
interested and . . . well, we want to eliminate anyone
who might present an obvious security risk. They have to
be suitable."

"And if they aren't suitable?"

"Then they'll never know or suspect anything," Ray said.

"And if there is reason to think they might be good
recruits, do we tell them right away?"

"Not us, and not then. We'll already have all their
addresses from the entry forms. If we want to pursue
them, we send another agent out to their homes to
continue the discussion in a more direct manner," Ray
explained. "So today we just have casual chit-chat . . . me
and my nephew from Canada."

"Don't you mean nephews? And who are you going to say Louise is?"

"Do you think they'll be with us?"

"Why wouldn't they?" I asked.

"I might think the two of them would prefer not to have us around. Two's company, three's a crowd . . . and four of us would make it even more crowded! But we'll see," Ray said.

"My mother would kill Jack if he went somewhere without me."

"Yes, but there'd be no harm if the two of them went off on their own for an hour or so while we're at the tournament, and your mother would never know . . . unless somebody told her."

I wouldn't do that and Ray knew it. Jack probably knew that too. I just wondered if he was thinking the same thing as Ray.

There was nothing to do now but sit back, wait and watch the scenery unfold outside the window on the way to London.

CHAPTER SIXTEEN

THE RAILWAY LINE naturally gave us a view of the worst of the devastation caused by the German bombing. The railroads themselves were targets—crucial for transportation of troops and supplies—but the tracks also ran past the factories that were the primary targets of the attacks.

As we got closer to London we saw more and more buildings that were bombed and burned-out hulks. There were stretches where everything, as far as the eye could see, had been reduced to rubble. In my mind I could picture how this had all happened—the drone of the Nazi bombers overhead, the whistling as the bombs rained down, the explosions lighting up the night, fires and dev-astation and death.

Instinctively I looked up at the sky. Clear, blue, nothing but a few fluffy white clouds and a few fluttering birds. I was so glad I was travelling during the day and would be gone long before nighttime came, bringing the threat of bombers with it. They came only at night. The only question mark was *which* nights. On some nights the bombers never arrived. On other nights they targeted different cities—Birmingham, Manchester and industrial centres throughout the country. On the worst nights, I'd heard it was as if the entire German air force was aimed right at the heart of London.

The train rumbled and bumped as it chugged through the yard and pulled into the station. The station's roof had collapsed in places, punctured by bombs, and the walls were blackened by fires, but it was still standing, just like the rest of London—just like the rest of England. Struck and bloodied and staggering but still on its feet, fighting back, unwilling to go down for the count.

The platform was filled with people, many of them in uniform. The people and the city had survived the Blitz, the worst that the Germans could throw at them, and though the bombing continued, they were still getting on with their lives.

The train shuddered to a stop and passengers got to their feet, gathered their possessions and started to exit.

I stood up but Ray put a hand on my shoulder. "Give 'em a minute to clear out."

We sat and waited while other people flocked off, and then Jack and Louise showed up at our compartment.

"Louise, I think you've been introduced to Ray, haven't you?" Jack said.

"Not formally," Ray answered, standing up. "But of course I know who young Louise is."

"Thank you for bringing Jack and George to London and allowing me to join you," she said.

"It's my pleasure. It's not every day that I get to entertain royalty." Ray bowed from the waist.

"Although we were hoping," Jack said, "if you wouldn't mind, if the two of us could . . . well . . ."

"Go off a bit on your own?" Ray asked.

"Just for a while," Louise said.

"And what exactly would you expect me to say to your parents?" Ray demanded of her.

"Well . . . I guess . . . do you think you'll be speaking to them?"

"Because you cannot expect me to lie," Ray went on. "Lying to a member of the royal family is practically treason."

"I'm so sorry," Louise said. "Please understand that we didn't mean to put you in such an awkward position. I didn't imagine . . . Please accept my sincere apologies."

"There's no need to apologize," Ray said. "But I do insist that you both accompany us to the chess tournament this morning."

"Yes, sir," Jack said.

"And then, when I'm *very* occupied, the two of you could possibly slip out, sort of unseen, and nobody would even notice," Ray said. "I know that *I* certainly wouldn't notice. Would you, George?"

"Trust me, I always pay as little attention to Jack as possible."

"But you can only count on me being occupied for two

hours, at most." He paused. "But of course if I'm ever invited to have tea with the King of England and your parents are there I just might have to let the cat out of the bag."

"Do you really think you could be invited . . ." Jack let the sentence trail off. He knew what Ray was saying—there was no chance of that ever happening.

Louise smiled. "Thank you so much!" She reached up and gave Ray a kiss on the cheek.

"Yeah, thanks," Jack said.

"Aren't you going to give me a little kiss too?" Ray asked, and then burst into laughter at the look on Jack's face. "Just kidding. Never let anybody say that old Ray got himself in the way of love. Now let's get moving. The sooner we get there, the sooner the two of you can disappear."

We followed Ray off the train—which was now almost empty—onto the platform and then into the station. It was filled with people who seemed to be in a rush, and there was a lot of jostling but nobody seemed upset. Instead, it was the opposite. There were smiles and laughter, good-natured conversation, people hugging and shaking hands. It was exciting to be there—I only wished we'd had somebody there to greet us.

"Is it far, wherever this chess thing is?" Jack asked.

"We'll take the Tube several stops headed north, and then—" Ray skidded to a stop. "Turn around, we're going to go another way."

He spun around, leaving us behind. We had to scramble to try to catch up to him. When he looked back at us he seemed shaken, bothered . . . no, wait, he wasn't looking back at us, he was looking *beyond* us. I turned around but didn't see anything that would be a worry.

"Ray!" Jack yelled. "Wait up!"

Ray glanced over his shoulder again. He now looked more concerned, and instead of stopping he was moving faster. He took a quick turn and disappeared from view down a station corridor. We rushed after him, and he was standing right there, waiting in the empty hallway.

"Keep going!" he hissed. "Quickly, keep walking!"

"But why? What's happening?"

"Keep moving and don't look back. There's no time for questions, just get out of here!"

There was a look of desperation, almost panic, in his

eyes. I didn't know what was wrong but it was serious, and I knew there wasn't time to think or talk or argue.

"Keep going and—"

"Hello, Ray." Three large men had come around the corner of the corridor. They were dressed well, in nice-looking suits, but their faces were menacing. A chill went up my spine.

"Fancy meeting you here," one of them said.

"Bruno, what a lucky coincidence," Ray said, a big smile on his face. "I was coming to see you."

The man, Bruno, laughed. "Yeah, right, I'm sure you were. And who are these three?"

"Nobody, I just met them on the train. They followed me off because I said I'd help them with directions. Let me just finish that piece of business and send them on their way . . . If you go out that door and turn to the left, a few blocks farther on you'll find that address you were asking me about. Nice to meet you. You'll be fine on your own now, and I'll just stay and talk to my friends here."

I nodded. "Yeah, thanks, mister. We'll just be going—"

"Nobody is going anywhere," Bruno said.

"These kids have nothing to do with our business," Ray said.

"Do you expect me to believe that?"

Who was he? He had an English accent, so clearly he wasn't a Nazi agent . . . or was he? I inched a little closer to Jack, who had pulled Louise tight and had his arm protectively around her.

"I told you, I just met them and gave them directions. We shared a train compartment. They're tourists . . . can't you tell by their accents?"

"So you expect us to believe that you don't know them?"

"Like I said, I just met them on the train."

"And they don't mean anything to you?" Bruno asked.

"Nothing. Just let them go," Ray said.

"If they don't mean anything, maybe I could just take care of them here and now."

"No, you can't do that!" Ray protested.

"We can't let them go, so they have to come with us."

"Look, buddy, I don't know who you are, but it's a free country and we can go anywhere we want," Jack said.

The man smiled—no, it wasn't a smile, it was a sneer. "You're not going anywhere, sonny-bob."

"Just let them go. I'm really sorry that—"

"Not as sorry as you're going to be, Ray," the man said. Suddenly a gun appeared in his hand. "We're going for a ride. *All* of us."

CHAPTER SEVENTEEN

WE WALKED OUT of the station as a group, with the biggest of the three men leading the way. Jack and Louise walked behind him, then me and Ray, and the other two followed after. All three made sure we knew they had guns and weren't afraid to use them.

"Look, I don't know what this is about," Jack said.

"Shut up, now!" Bruno snapped. "Not another word. And don't even think about running."

"Just do as he says," Ray told us. Ray looked frightened, which made me feel afraid.

We stopped at the curb, and a big, black, fancy car came roaring up and then skidded to a stop beside us.

It reminded me of the car that had brought us from the port to Bletchley.

The big man opened the back door and gestured for us to get inside. Jack hesitated and then was shown the gun once again. There was no choice. He climbed in, followed by Louise, me, then Ray and the other men. The door was slammed shut and Bruno climbed into the front passenger seat. Once again we were in a car with the windows blackened so that we couldn't see out and nobody could see in.

I worked hard to settle my mind, to try not to let my fear overwhelm my thoughts. Louise was working hard to be brave but I could tell that she was on the verge of tears, and she was shaking. She clutched Jack's hand. She was scared, and had good reason to be. Who were these men?

All of them were in dark suits and ties and wore fedoras and well-polished shoes, as though they were just businessmen on their way to the office. They spoke with English accents—accents that were very similar to Ray's and very different from Louise's. I had to get them talking to get more information, to try to figure out what they wanted and who they were. If they were "friends" of Ray's it probably meant they were thugs, criminals. That was good . . . well, at least better than Nazi agents.

"Excuse me," I said. "Where are you taking us?"

"You'll find out soon enough." It was always Bruno who spoke. He was obviously in charge.

"Who are these people?" I asked Ray.

He looked a bit uncomfortable and then answered, "I guess you could call them former business associates."

"Business associates?" Bruno laughed. "Isn't that just la-di-da, upper crust. We worked on jobs together."

"The last one was the job that got me arrested and jailed," Ray said.

"But you're not in jail now."

"Look, I didn't sell you out if that's what you're getting at. You know that, because if I had you'd all be in jail now."

"We know you didn't sell us out," he said. "We also know about the deal you made to get out of jail."

I knew the deal—release from jail in exchange for putting his special talents to use by the government— but did they know that?

"So what exactly do you do for those government people?" Bruno asked.

Even if they didn't know exactly, they certainly knew some of it.

"If you know that much, you know I can't tell you anything else," Ray said.

"You'll tell us what we want to hear, one way or another." Bruno spoke quietly, which made his threat sound so much more dangerous. "Whatever it is, it must be important," he went on. "We know you have clearance to go in and out of pretty well every building in the city."

"How do you know that?" Ray asked.

"We have eyes and we have connections. Do you think there's anything that goes on in this city without me knowing something about it one way or another?"

"How much?" Ray asked. "How much money do you want to let us go?"

"What makes you think this is about money?" he asked.

"Isn't it always about money?" Ray asked.

"I guess it is, and believe me, you're worth a lot more to us than any money you could ever raise."

"Then what do you want from me?"

"To get that money, we are in need of your special talents."

"All right, I'm beginning to get the picture. What do you want me to do?" Ray asked.

"There is a certain safe that contains something we need, or more accurately something we need to sell for a lot of money, a mountain of money."

"And that's all you want?" Ray asked. "If there's lots of money, I'm in. You can let the other three go now and I'll do it."

"We'll keep the three of them as our guests until you bring it back, and then we'll let you all go."

"How do I know that you'll keep your word? How do I know if I bring it back you won't just put a bullet into each of us?"

"I guess you don't," Bruno said. "Just do what I'm telling you to do."

"And if I don't?"

"I dump four bodies on the side of the road and drive away." He pulled his gun out and aimed it directly at my head! "Well, which is it going to be?"

"Wait just a second, not so fast. If this is business, then

we need to negotiate a little before I make my decision," Ray said.

"How about if I kill the kid just to show you that you're not in a position to negotiate?" He pulled back the hammer of the gun and panic filled my body.

"If you kill the kid you get nothing," Ray said defiantly. "If you negotiate you get 85 percent of what you want."

"Did you say 85 percent?"

"Yeah, don't I deserve a little taste of what's in this? Is 15 percent too much for my troubles and talents?"

The man laughed. "I thought you worked for the government."

"I do, but the pay ain't too great. Well, do you want me as a partner?"

Was Ray really going to sell us out, or was he just pretending? I tried to catch his eye, to get a hint of what he was doing, but he was staring straight at Bruno, almost as if he was avoiding looking at me.

"You always did have a lot of nerve," Bruno said.

"You can't do what I do for a living if you don't. Well, do we have a deal, or are you going to shoot the lad?"

For an instant I'd somehow forgotten there was a gun

pointed at me! I looked directly at it, straight down the barrel.

Bruno gave another one of those sinister smiles and lowered the gun. "Okay, 10 percent. Take it or leave it."

"That's the first part," Ray said. "You know that once this happens I'm going to be a wanted man, so you'll have to use your connections to get me out of the country."

"After this job we're *all* going to leave the country."

"Then I think we have a deal I can live with," Ray said.

"That's good to know, because it means these three kids can live too." He lowered the pistol completely. "You're going to make me very rich."

"Am I breaking into the Royal Mint?"

"Actually, you're not far off."

The car swerved and then slowed down and came to a stop.

"Perfect timing, we're here. And be assured that if any of you try to escape or screw up I will not only kill you, but I will do so in a very slow, painful manner."

There was a look on his face that was almost joyful, as if he was actually hoping that we'd screw up so that he could follow through with the threat.

"Out."

We were ushered out of the car and into a narrow alley, with a warehouse on one side and a huge pile of rubble on the other where a building, presumably, had stood before the bombing. The far end of the alley was piled high with more rubble, and two of the men stood blocking the exit to the street. There was no place to run.

Bruno opened a door and we went into the building, with the fourth man, the driver, leading the way.

Stepping inside I hesitated, my eyes adjusting to the limited light. We were hurried down two flights of stairs and through another door. I stopped. It was damp and chilly. There were gigantic hooks hanging from the ceiling—we were in what must have been some sort of meat locker.

I was shoved from behind. "Keep it moving," Bruno ordered. I stumbled forward.

"No need to be rough with them," Ray said.

"You been gone a long time if you think that was rough," Bruno said, and the other three laughed. "You three sit down over there." He directed us to some old wooden chairs lined up against the wall.

Jack took Louise by the hand. She looked as terrified as I felt, but I couldn't show it. Neither could Jack. He was putting on a brave front, placing his arm around her shoulders, trying to protect her. I couldn't even think about her or Jack. I had to pay attention to what was going on and hope I could find a way out.

"I want you to treat the kids well," Ray said.

"I am going to treat them really well. They're living, breathing insurance against you deciding to do something stupid like not bringing me back the goods."

"I'll bring you back the goods," Ray said.

"I'm sure *they* are even gladder than I am to hear you say it."

"It's going to be okay," Jack whispered to Louise. "I won't let anybody hurt you."

"So how long do we have before somebody notices you're gone?" Bruno asked Ray.

"Probably no later than six this evening."

"I guess that means we're going to have to do it today."

"That's not enough time to plan a full-scale heist," Ray said.

"It's not that big, and not that full-scale," Bruno said.

"You said this haul would make us all rich. What sort of safe holds that much loot without having proper security?" Ray asked.

"It has security, but I've seen you walk in there with my own eyes," Bruno said.

"What is it exactly that you want me to steal?" Ray asked.

"It's not so much 'steal' as 'borrow,'" Bruno said. "You're just taking pictures."

"Pictures of what?"

"I'll tell you all about it . . . but in private." Bruno stood up and started to walk away.

"Hold on," Ray said. Bruno stopped. "I just want to talk to my friends."

"We don't have time for that," Bruno said.

But Ray didn't listen. He just walked over until he was standing in front of us.

"I don't want any of you to do anything stupid." He looked directly at Jack and then at me.

I nodded my head in agreement.

"Look," Bruno yelled. "Don't worry. We're going to lock the three of them up so they're safe and sound. They won't have a chance to do anything stupid. Now *we* need to talk."

He walked out of the room and Ray followed. Just before he left Ray turned around and gave us a reassuring look. It didn't help.

The other three men followed them out of the room, leaving us alone.

"We are going to be all right, aren't we?" Louise whimpered.

"We're going to be fine," Jack said. When he hugged her his face was turned toward me, and his expression told a very different story. He knew we were far from "fine."

He ended the hug and then took both of her hands in his, and now he looked her square in the eyes. "You have to understand that George and I have been in worse pickles than this, and we've always gotten out of them. We'll get out of this."

Her lower lip was quivering, but she was trying hard for that "stiff upper lip" that would stop her from crying.

"Do you trust me?" Jack said.

She nodded her head ever so slightly.

"Good ol' Ray will do what they want, bring back whatever they want, and then they'll let us all go."

When he said it out loud like that it became painfully obvious to me that it *wasn't* going to happen that way. We'd seen their faces. We even knew Bruno's name. Would they let us go knowing full well that we could identify them and get them arrested for kidnapping and robbery? I knew the answer to that, and I figured Jack knew it too. I just hoped Ray understood it as well. Our best hope was that he would get out there and get us the help we'd need to get free. Of course he'd figure it out and do what was needed. Unless that 10 percent was too much for him to turn down. I guess we'd soon find out if my mother was right about him—could a leopard change its spots?

Three men walked back in. Where were Bruno and Ray? One of them pulled a pair of handcuffs out of his pocket and tossed them to Jack.

"Put them on," he snarled.

"Say please," Jack said.

"What did you say?"

"I said, say plea—"

The man reached out and smacked Jack across the face, sending him flying out of the chair and onto the cement floor! Louise screamed, and I jumped to my feet.

The man pulled out his gun.

"Is that polite enough for you, mate?" the man yelled. He turned to me. "Pick him up!"

I bent down beside Jack. "Are you okay?"

"I've been hit harder," he said, looking directly at the man, challenging him to hit him again.

"Shut up," I hissed at him.

"Better do what your brother says," the man said threateningly. "Unless you want to see if I *can* hit you harder."

"He doesn't," I said. I grabbed the handcuffs off the floor, and before Jack could argue I snapped them on his wrists.

"What are you doing?"

"Stopping you from making things worse." I pulled Jack to his feet and then pushed him back into his chair.

"Now put these on her," the man said as he handed me another set of cuffs.

I bent down in front of Louise. "I'm sorry."

She nodded her head. Those tears she'd been trying to hold back were leaking out now.

"And you know what these are for," he said as he handed me a third pair.

I snapped a cuff on one of my wrists and then the other. We were all cuffed.

As I sat back down Bruno and Ray came back into the room. Ray looked at the cuffs and then at Jack. His face was already swollen, and there was blood seeping from his lip.

"What happened here?" Ray shouted.

"He had a little accident," the big gorilla said.

Ray turned to Bruno. "I thought we had a deal!"

"We do."

"The deal is that I get you what you want and you don't harm them. Does that look like nobody was harmed?"

"It won't happen again," Bruno said.

"You know, even if I did believe you, there's no way I trust that goon." Ray pointed at the big guy who had hit Jack. "I'm not going anywhere if he stays here."

"That's not going to be a problem," Bruno said. "Dom's going with you. All three of my men are going with you."

"I can't take them into the Naval Intelligence offices."

Did he just say Naval Intelligence? There wouldn't be anything very valuable there—except for information. Information about Enigma and Shark and Dolphin. And that information would only be valuable to the Nazis.

"They won't be going in with you. They'll drive you there and wait outside. I'm going to wait here with the kids."

"That's better," Ray said.

"Perhaps. You need to know that if there's a problem of any kind—if you don't get what we need, if you alert anybody, if there are any hitches—they'll let me know, and believe me, I *will* kill them. You know me, Ray ol' friend."

His voice was calm, quiet, determined. This wasn't a threat, it was a promise.

"Look, mate, you know there's nothing to worry about." Ray turned to face us. "Nothing to worry about . . . do you understand?"

I should have felt reassured, but I didn't. Was he just saying that to keep us from trying anything because he was now part of the deal?

"It's time to get going," Bruno said.

"You're right. It's important to *pick* the right time," Ray said.

He was answering Bruno but he was looking straight at me. There was no mistaking the emphasis on "pick"—I had my pick with me, and he knew it. Ray was telling me something. He wanted me to try to escape . . . was that what he was saying?

I noticed then that Ray was holding his special pen—the one that Ian had given him, the gun pen. He wasn't going to use it, was he? That would make no sense. It had only one bullet and there were four of them. He wiggled it and then looked directly at me and nodded ever so slightly. I nodded back. He wanted to know if I'd seen it.

"So we'd better get going," Ray said. Carefully, casually, he put the pen down on the edge of a table. He was leaving it, and there was only one reason for that—he was leaving it for me to use. He looked directly at me and gave me one more nod—approval to do what I needed to do.

CHAPTER EIGHTEEN

I SHIFTED UNEASILY in my chair. In the meat locker that we were being held in were a number of floor-to-ceiling poles that must have been needed for structural support, and before the men had left they'd moved each of our chairs so that it was beside one and then rearranged our cuffs, looping the chain around the poles to lock us in place with our arms in front of us.

I had one eye on Bruno, sitting at the table reading the paper, and a second on the pen sitting there innocently beside him. I looked at my watch. It was almost noon—three hours since they'd left, and five or six hours before anybody would expect us to be back or even begin to think that something was wrong. Even then, what would they do? How would they know where to look? If we were getting out of this, it was going to be because of something that we did—us and Ray. I knew Ray could be trusted. He had left that pen for a reason. I just had to get to it.

"I'm getting hungry," I said.

"Not as hungry as you're going to be."

"I guess we're all going to be hungry."

He pulled an apple out of his pocket and took a big bite. "Maybe not all of us." He chewed, swallowed and took another big bite, all the time staring at me, enjoying the taunting.

"How long do you think this is going to take?" I asked.

"If it works, he'll be back within a few hours, by dark at the latest."

"And then we'll be free to go?" I asked.

"Then we'll leave."

"And we'll be free?"

"Yeah, then you'll be free."

I knew he was lying. He wasn't going to set us free. The best we could hope for was that they would leave us chained down here while they made their getaway, left the country. If they did that, I could pick the cuffs and get us free. It might take me a while but I could do it.

"You didn't run into Ray just by chance, did you," I said.

He took another bite from the apple, slowly chewed and then swallowed. "We've been looking for him for a while, and we'd been told that he went through that train station regularly. We were waiting for him."

"There has to be more than one safecracker in London. You needed him because he could get into a place that nobody else could, Naval Intelligence."

"Why should I talk to you about any of this?" he asked.

"Why shouldn't you? It's not like I'm going anywhere."

He laughed. "No, you're not." He took another bite. "Yeah, he was the only one we knew who could get into Naval Intelligence headquarters. It's not like they normally let in the common folk and the criminal element, but Ray seems to be able to go wherever he wants."

"Why would you want him to go there?" Jack asked. "They don't have anything valuable."

"Information can be very valuable . . . to the right buyer."

"The only people who would want that information are the Nazis," Jack said.

"Their money is as good as anybody else's."

"How can you work with the enemy?" Jack questioned.

"I'll work with whoever has the most money."

"You're a traitor," Jack spat.

"I'm a businessman."

"You're English, how can you betray your own country?" Louise asked.

"My country? How long do you think there will even be an England?"

"We're going to win this war," she said.

"That's what I keep hearing in those speeches. But I'd rather have guns and planes and tanks than pithy speeches."

"Some people would rather die with honour than live with dishonour," Jack said.

Bruno laughed. "You sound like a schoolboy! Well, you can have your honourable death since it means so much to you. Me, I'll be sitting on a beach somewhere far away from here, living the good life."

"You're not leaving any witnesses behind, are you?" I asked.

"You'll be alive when I leave," Bruno said.

"But for how much longer?" I asked. I'd been thinking that and wanted to see if he'd answer, what his reaction would be.

His smirk grew ever so slightly, and his eyes seemed to glow brighter, as if he was looking forward to what was going to happen to us. That could only mean something awful. I needed to know more. I had to get him talking.

"So you're just going to walk up to them and exchange the plans for some money," I said.

"Not *some* money, a king's ransom. Besides, nobody is going to be walking. It's all going to happen two blocks from here. I'll drive my car behind the church and at midnight we make the exchange."

"Maybe they'll just shoot you and take what they want. There's no honour among thieves, or spies."

"Those Nazis are businessmen, just like me," Bruno said. "Besides, my men will be close by with weapons in hand. I'm not taking any chances." He tossed the apple core into a garbage can and snatched the pen from the desk, pointing it directly at us! Did he know it was a gun?

"And you're just going to leave us here, alive," Jack said.

"As I told you, when I leave you'll be alive, but this is a dangerous part of London. Bombs drop around here almost every night."

"You're going to just leave us here and hope we get bombed?" Jack asked.

That would work for me. We'd get loose after they left.

"No hope involved," Bruno said. "See those cans in the corner?"

We all looked over. There were a number of large drums.

"Those are filled with petrol. There's a small explosive with a timer on them. If I start the timer this whole building will go up. And you know what? In a city under constant bombing, nobody will think it's anything but a Nazi bomb. Down here, two storeys below, buried in rubble, they won't find your remains for weeks, maybe months."

"You never had any intention of letting us go," I said. "You're just a lying traitor."

"You should shut up now or I won't be waiting for any bomb to go off."

I knew I'd pushed him as far as he could be pushed without him pushing back. He picked up the newspaper again and flipped through the pages until he came to the crossword puzzle. He turned away from us. He started reading the clues and tried to ink in the first answer.

"Louise," I hissed softly. "Ask to go to the washroom."

She nodded softly. She was scared but she was trying to be brave.

"Excuse me," she called out. "I have to use the facilities."

Bruno turned around. "Hold it."

"I can't. Please . . . I'm not going to try anything . . . please."

He gave a loud sigh and then got up. He walked over and undid one of the cuffs, pulling her to her feet.

"You'd better not harm her," Jack said.

"How sweet, and how pathetic." He pulled out his gun and aimed it right at Jack's head. "Anything more you want to say?"

Jack shook his head.

"If either of you two try anything you won't have to wait to die."

He led Louise across the room and then out the door at the end. I heard their footfalls leading away.

"If he hurts her I'll——"

"Shut up," I hissed.

Awkwardly I fumbled around in my coat pocket, trying to grab the pick. The cuffs made it hard but not impossible. I grabbed it and pulled it free. Quickly I flipped over the cuffs to reveal the lock. I inserted the tip of my pick into the opening.

"Hurry up," Jack said.

"Again, shut up and listen for him coming back."

I'd never tried to pick handcuffs. I figured they wouldn't be very different from a lock on a door—except the door wasn't attached to my wrist. I closed my eyes. That always made it easier to feel the pick against the lock and—*click*—it popped open!

"Get mine off," Jack hissed.

I stumbled to my feet, the cuff and chain still attached to one hand, and bent down over Jack to undo his cuffs. And then I heard steps coming back down the hall. There wouldn't be time for me to get his cuffs off. I turned and ran across the room and grabbed the pen from the table. If I ran to the door and surprised him I could get in a shot—and maybe get us all killed if that one shot didn't work. I ran back across the room, shoved the pen in my sock and reattached myself to the pole, clicking the cuffs locked again. A couple of seconds later they walked back into the room. Bruno brought Louise over and clicked on the cuffs around the pole.

"Thank you," Louise said.

"Yeah, sure. And if anybody else needs to go you can do it in your pants."

I looked over at Jack. His expression was complete shock. He must have thought I'd lost my mind. He didn't know that the pen was a gun, and I really couldn't tell him.

Bruno settled back into the chair, picked up his newspaper and started looking around the top of the table— he was searching for the missing pen. He moved the paper around and then bent over and looked on the floor. Of course, unless he searched my sock he wasn't going to find it. Hopefully he'd think he'd dropped it somewhere on the way to the bathroom.

Now there was nothing to do but keep my eyes open and wait for the right moment, and pray that moment would come. It wasn't just that this little gun had only one shot—*we* had only one shot at escape.

Bruno was slumped in the chair, his feet up on the table and his back to us, snoring. It had started as a gentle whistle and was now a deep, loud rumble.

I leaned as close to Jack as I could. "Jack," I whispered. "The pen." I pointed down at my sock. "It's a gun."

"What?"

I looked over at Bruno to make sure he was still asleep. "A gun . . . it's a gun."

"Shoot him."

"Can't. He's too far away . . . it only has one bullet."

Jack nodded. "Pick the lock and get closer."

I nodded my head. I could do that. Pick the lock, sneak over and then shoot him while he slept . . . shooting a sleeping man . . . could I do that?

Slowly I reached into my pocket for my pick— Bruno yawned loudly, stretched and started moving. I pulled my hand out of my pocket. He yawned again and got to his feet.

"We could be here another five or six hours," Bruno said. "I'm not an animal, and I'm sorry that I have to treat you lot like animals."

Why was he saying that? Why was he being nice? That was more scary than reassuring.

"Even animals are given some food and water," Jack said. "And it's only decent to let your prisoners go to the washroom."

Bruno actually did look sorry. But then he pulled out his gun and walked toward us.

"You first," he said to Jack and tossed him the keys to the cuffs.

"You can't kill him!" I exclaimed.

Bruno laughed. "I could kill 'im, easy as pie, but I'm not going to kill 'im. Unlock the cuffs and I'll take you to the washroom, give you a drink of water. Then I'll lock 'im back up and do the other two of you."

"Thank you," Louise said.

"No problem. Why can't you two have manners like

this one? And just so you know, I will plug you if you even sneeze wrong. Understand?"

Jack nodded.

There was a noise from the stairwell. We all heard it. Bruno spun around, his gun now aimed at the closed door.

"It's me!" came a voice through the door. It was Ray. "I'm coming in!"

Slowly the door opened and Ray walked in, his hands in the air. "Is it all right for me to put my arms down?"

"Did you get it?" Bruno demanded.

"I got it. It all went according to plan . . . well, at least for me."

"What do you mean?" Bruno asked.

"You might have noticed I'm alone."

"Where are my men?"

"Let's just say we have three less partners to cut in on the action," Ray said.

"They were captured?"

Ray laughed. "They were killed."

"By you?" Bruno looked and sounded shocked.

"Do you think you're the only one with connections?

My two associates are waiting upstairs, guarding the entrance."

"And they killed all three of them?" Bruno asked.

"Two. I plugged Dom myself."

"You've never killed anybody before," Bruno said.

"War changes people. Besides, him I enjoyed killing."

"So what now?" Bruno asked.

"We rethink our partnership. You get 50 percent, I get 50 percent," Ray said. "We both need what the other has. You have the connection and I have the product."

"And what about them?" Bruno asked, pointing at us.

"What about them?" Ray asked.

"You know we can't let them go," Bruno said.

"I know you never planned on letting them go. What's going to happen to them?"

"An explosion timed for tonight. No survivors."

"Smart. We walk away and whatever happens, happens," Ray said.

"And you're okay with that?" Bruno asked.

"Better them than me. Besides, you know my jail time hasn't been erased, just postponed. As soon as this war is over I'm back in the can for another ten years. Excuse me if I'd rather be serving that time somewhere far away."

Was Ray really selling us out, or was he agreeing just to save us? He knew I had my pick and could get out of the cuffs if I was left alone for a while . . . unless he was going to take that away from me before he left.

Bruno lowered the gun. "Before I agree to anything, how do I know that you even have the plans?"

Ray reached into his pocket and pulled out what looked like a little camera. "I have in here the invasion plans for Europe. Full and complete and worth more money than you and I could ever use if we lived to be two hundred."

Bruno raised the gun again. "And what's to stop me from simply shooting you and taking the plans?"

"I told you, my men are upstairs guarding the entrance. You walk out without me and you won't get more than two steps," Ray said.

Bruno nodded his head. "It sounds like you've thought everything out . . . well . . . almost everything."

"What do you mean?" Ray asked.

"You said *entrance*. A rat always has at least two ways out of his lair. Ideally, one of them is one that nobody else knows about." Bruno raised the gun and pointed it directly at Ray. "I'll take that camera now."

"But . . . but we had a deal," Ray said. "We're partners . . . how about if I go back to taking 10 percent?"

"I'm afraid I have a better offer for you. I get 100 percent and you get dead."

There was a sudden scraping noise beside me and Jack went flying through the air, crashing into Bruno. The gun went off as the two of them tumbled to the ground!

The gun clattered across the floor as Jack and Bruno rolled around in a ball! Jack had unlocked his cuffs— Bruno had given him the key and then forgotten about him when Ray came in! The gun was free, all Ray had to do was pick it up and— Ray was lying on his back, motionless. I could see blood seeping out of his side— he'd been shot!

Jack and Bruno rolled around and exchanged punches, all arms and legs, knees and fists! I had to help him, but I was chained in place. The two faced off against each other. Bruno was bigger but Jack was a scrapper—I'd seen him beat bigger guys more than once.

There was a flash of metal from Bruno's hands and

instantly I knew what it was—he was holding a knife. That same sick smile came to his face and he started to chuckle.

"I'm going to fillet you like a fish, boy. You're gonna regret ever doing what you did."

Jack backed up, staggered by the appearance of the knife. Desperately he looked around for something he could use as a weapon. If only he could get to the gun. It was off to the side and there was no way he could reach it—Bruno and his knife stood in the way. But there was one gun that I could get to.

I pulled the pen out of my sock as Bruno slowly stalked toward Jack. I pulled back the clip and aimed at him, but he was on the other side of the room, too far for me to have any chance at accuracy. And I was still cuffed to the pole. I only had the one shot, and if I missed we were all dead.

"Jack!" I yelled.

He looked over, and in that instant he saw that I was holding the pen. He knew what to do. He faked to the left and then dropped down to one knee as Bruno lunged at him. The blade just missed, slicing over his head. Jack rolled, over and over, toward me, Bruno desperately chasing him, trying to stab him with the blade. Jack slammed into a pole and Bruno pounced on him, raised the knife to plunge it into Jack's side—and I fired.

CHAPTER NINETEEN

BRUNO'S ARM—knife in hand—remained in the air, suspended above Jack. Then he turned, looked at me and smiled. It wasn't a sneer or a smirk but almost a genuine smile. Bruno laughed, dropped the knife and clutched his chest before he tumbled over to one side.

Jack, a look of terror on his face, scrambled backward like a crab. "He's . . . he's shot," he stammered.

"Jack, are you all right?" Louise called.

"Get the gun and get us loose!" I yelled.

Jack hesitated for an instant, frozen, unable to decide which of the two things to do first. At last he clambered to his feet and came toward us, key in hand to unlock the cuffs. It was over, we were free, we were safe and—

The door smashed open and Bruno's men came running into the room, guns drawn! How was that possible? They were dead and . . . no, these weren't Bruno's goons! I recognized the first man—it was Ian! And right behind him was my father! They weren't thugs, they were the good guys coming to the rescue!

"Ray's been shot!" I called out.

"Get a medic!" Ian yelled. He dropped to his knee beside Ray and lifted up his head. Ray reacted with a loud, clear groan. He wasn't dead, but it didn't look good.

My father rushed over and helped steady Jack on his feet.

"Jack, are you okay? And Louise?"

"We're okay, just a bit shaken up."

"And roughed up, by the looks of it. Ian, what about Ray?"

Ray lifted his head with a grimace. "I think I'll live . . . thanks to Jack."

My father turned to me. "And you're all right?"

"I will be if somebody uncuffs me."

"Sorry, get them loose," Ian ordered.

"I have the keys," Jack called out. He unlocked Louise's cuffs and she threw her arms around him and burst into tears as they hugged.

"Hey, aren't you forgetting somebody?" I yelled.

With one arm still around Louise he tossed me the keys and I caught them. Quickly I unlocked the cuffs, freeing myself from the pole. I rushed over to Ray's side.

"Ray, are you all right?" I exclaimed.

"Of course I'm *not* all right," Ray said. "I've been shot, in case you hadn't noticed."

"Shut up and just lie back," Ian said. "Help is coming . . . you're going to be just fine."

"And what makes you such a medical expert?" Ray demanded.

"I'm no expert, but dying people aren't usually so talkative. Besides, I can see it's just a nick—it got more of your clothing than it did you."

Ray sat up and looked at his side. There was a clear red

gash but it looked more like a deep scratch than a bullet wound.

"Nothing fatal about this," Ian said.

"It still hurts like hell," Ray said. "Bruno . . . is he dead?"

Ian turned to my father, who was kneeling beside Bruno.

"No signs of life," my father said. "He's gone."

"That's terrible!" Ray exclaimed.

I hadn't expected him to be upset about the man who shot him being dead.

"I got shot for nothing!"

"I didn't mean to kill him," I sputtered.

"You didn't have any choice," Jack said. "If you hadn't shot him he would have killed me."

"But still . . . I don't understand what happened," I said. "Why is everybody here?"

"As soon as Ray got to Naval Intelligence he found me and told me about the plan," Ian said.

"They phoned me at Bletchley and I came down on the next train," my father said.

"And my parents?" Louise asked. "They think I'm visiting a school friend. They'll be wondering why I'm not home."

"Your parents have been notified," Ian said. "I imagine you—and Jack—will have some explaining to do."

"But what about Bruno's men?" I asked. "What happened to them?"

"We arranged for them to be captured," Ian explained.

"So you didn't kill them?" Jack asked.

"Me? I've never killed anybody in my whole life," Ray said.

"No, we captured them without a fight," Ian said. "Which was good, because we didn't want any bullet holes in their suits."

"Why *are* you dressed in their clothes?" I asked.

"In case this building was being watched by Nazi agents," Ian explained. "We didn't want to tip them off that we were on to what they were doing. We were going to give Bruno the invasion plans to sell to the Nazis."

"But they can't get those plans!" I exclaimed.

"We were giving him *false* plans," Ray said.

"Remember the Haversack Ruse? We were going to give them the fake plans we've been working on at Naval

Intelligence for the past six months. All we lacked was a way to get the plans to them, and then this came up," Ian said. "Ray came back in here to give Bruno the false plans so that he'd sell them to the enemy agents."

"And now Bruno is dead," Ray said.

"And with his death, we've lost the opportunity to pass on false information to the enemy. If they had bought our ruse we could have saved thousands of lives," Ian said.

"I'm so sorry . . . I didn't have any choice . . . if I'd known," I stammered.

"There was no way to tell you. But knowing wouldn't have made any difference—you did what you had to do to save your brother's life," Ray said. "There's nothing we can do now. We don't even know his contact."

"I don't know his contact but we know when and where he was supposed to pass on the information," I said.

"You do?" Ray exclaimed.

"Bruno told us. I guess he figured it wasn't like we were going to tell anybody," Jack said. "He said it would happen at midnight in an alley, behind a church a couple of blocks from here."

"There are a lot of churches in this area," Ian said.

"But only one where we've ever made drop-offs," Ray said. "I know the church."

"What an excellent turn of events," Ian said. "We can't deliver the fake plan, but at least we can capture the enemy agents. It's something."

"What if I delivered the plans to them?" Ray asked.

"I appreciate the offer," Ian said, "but it wouldn't work."

"Why not?" Ray asked.

"I strongly suspect they're on to you being a government agent. They're probably the ones who tipped Bruno off to go looking for you," Ian said.

"I could convince them I've turned and only want the money. You know I'm a very convincing liar," Ray said. "I bet I even had these three convinced I was a traitor."

"I was beginning to wonder," Jack said.

"Me too," Louise agreed.

I shook my head. "Not me."

"Why not?" Ray asked.

"You left the pen, you knew I had a pick, and besides, I just knew we could trust you, even with our lives."

Ray struggled to get up, aided by Ian, and came right

over to me. "Thank you, for not just saying that but believing it."

"We'll get a detail in place to arrest the agents when they appear," Ian said. "Maybe we could turn them into double agents and get them to pass on the false plans that way. Not that I'd ever really trust a double agent. No, I think arresting them is our only realistic choice."

"Well," I said, "there is one other choice. What if Bruno did deliver the plan?"

"George, Bruno's dead," my father said. "He's not going to be delivering anything."

"I know he's dead," I said. "But that doesn't mean he can't make his meeting."

CHAPTER TWENTY

THE BIG BLACK CAR sat behind the church, in the spot where Ray figured Bruno would have waited. The engine was running—it had been running for the past forty minutes. Ian had driven it there extra early so the Nazi agents wouldn't see it arriving. Then he and my father had positioned Bruno's body in the driver's seat, slumped over the wheel, his left hand on the dashboard, the camera with the false plans in his right hand, visible to anybody who came up to the open window.

"What time is it?" I whispered.

Ian shifted his wrist to try to see his watch. "A little after midnight."

"They should have been here. Do you think they spotted us?"

"We were careful, and every one of my agents is safely hidden."

Ian, my father, two armed commandos and I were sitting in the dark at a window in a building overlooking the car. Ray had been taken away to get medical treatment, and Jack had gone with Louise to help keep her calm as she was returned to her no-doubt-furious parents. In spite of the danger, I was pretty sure I was safer in the alley with Ian and my father than Jack was in Windsor.

Two other commandos, with sniper rifles, were up high, hidden in the church belfry. Another dozen agents in cars were staked out around the drop site, ready to tail the enemy agents after they made the pickup—or even if they didn't. If they were suspicious they might leave without the camera, but Ian said his agents would still follow them and hope to be led to other spies. He said it was like "following a rat to its nest."

"I've got to tell you, George, I'm still not sure how you ever came up with the idea of a dead man delivering the package."

"I just thought about the Haversack Ruse," I said. "But instead of spies getting the goods from a living man, they could snatch what they wanted from the hands of a dead one," I said.

"It is brilliant," Ian said, "and you thought of it right there, on the spot."

"I just hope it will work."

"Do you hear something?" my father asked.

"Car engine," Ian said.

As we watched, a black shadow, the silhouette of a car, rolled slowly down the alley with its lights out. The only reason a car would travel without lights was that it didn't want to be seen. I felt the hair on the back of my neck rise up. It was going to happen.

The car came to a stop. Its lights flashed on and off, on and off.

"He's signalling," Ian said. "Bruno is probably supposed to signal back."

"And if he doesn't?" I asked.

"If it was me I'd just leave," Ian said. "But it all depends on how desperate they are for the information."

The car signalled again—clicked the lights on and off

twice—and again there was no response from Bruno. If he *had* responded I'd have been pretty worried, and more than a little spooked.

"This is the moment of truth," Ian said. "Come on, come on, don't be afraid, my little pretties."

The car moved forward, toward Bruno's vehicle. It stopped once again, no more than two car lengths away. The lights came on once again, this time to shine into Bruno's car. They couldn't avoid seeing him there at the wheel.

"Everybody hold your positions," Ian said into a small radio.

The lights went off again, and at the same time all four doors of the car opened and four men climbed out. Two of them walked cautiously toward Bruno's car, one on each side, and the other two fanned farther out. In the dark I couldn't see their features, but I assumed they had weapons drawn. One of them was carrying a small case—did that contain the money to be exchanged for the plans?

They looked in the window. They now had to know he was dead. They also probably saw the camera there in his hand. Would they just drive off, or would they take the bait? Would they think Bruno had been shot getting the plans, then drove up and died before they could make the drop?

I tried to put myself in that car, listening, watching for their reactions, trying to think the way they'd think. Me, I would have been suspicious, but still, I might have believed it because I *wanted* to believe it. We all knew how important these plans were. The success or failure of the invasion of Europe rested on surprise—either them surprising us by knowing when and where we were going to land our troops, or us surprising them by landing in another location, on another day.

One of the men leaned into the driver's window. Was he checking for a pulse, or reaching for the camera?

Suddenly the four men retreated and got back into their car. Almost the instant the four doors slammed shut, the car started up, reversing out of the alley, the engine whining as it picked up speed. The driver found a space wide enough to turn and he quickly spun the car around. The lights came on and it raced away.

"The rabbit is on the run," Ian said into the radio.

"Heading east from the alley. Pursue from a distance but do *not*, I repeat, *do not* apprehend or allow yourself to be seen!"

We all got to our feet. "What now?" I asked.

"Now we check to see if the bait was taken," Ian said.

We followed him out of the building and into the alley. It was a bit unnerving to be there so soon after the enemy. Almost as unnerving as thinking that they'd been allowed to leave and had not been arrested. Quietly we approached the car, as though we were sneaking up on Bruno, as though we didn't want to wake him up. Ian shone a flashlight into the open window.

"The camera is gone," he said.

"They took the bait!" I said.

"Does that mean they believe it?" my father asked.

"They wouldn't have taken the camera if they didn't think there was some reason to believe it," Ian said. "Of course, this is just the first step. Now we're going to help them believe."

"What else will you do?" I asked.

"We'll plant supporting stories with other agents, use double agents we've already turned, create fake documents and radio transmissions to support the facts of this invasion that won't happen. We're now going to *sell* the story . . . the story that you helped to deliver."

"In the end, do you think it will work?" my father asked.

"We won't know for sure for months and months, not until after the real invasion takes place," Ian said. "And we might never know how our actions here tonight worked or didn't work. One thing is certain, though: the roles we played today will be kept tightly under wraps."

"I understand," I said. "And as far as I'm concerned, I'd like all of this kept secret from at least one person in particular."

My father laughed. "I wouldn't count on that. Your mother already knows something's up. And she has her own ways of getting to the truth. She's bound to find out about it."

"All of it?" I asked.

"Actually, she won't be told any of it. Neither will Louise's parents. Besides those of us here tonight, this will be known by only a few other people in all of the

Allied command," Ian said. "People like Little Bill, the prime minister and the head of Naval Intelligence."

"It's probably best," my father said. "No need to worry your mother any further. In fact, we'd better be getting home now."

Ian put a hand on my shoulder. "George, someday—maybe in a few years, maybe not for a decade—this is all going to come to light, and people will know what you did, that you are a hero."

"Me, a hero?" I shook my head. "I'm just some twelve-year-old delivering mail at Bletchley Park. And speaking of that, we'd better get going . . . Mrs. Pruitt will kill me if I'm late for my shift."

AUTHOR'S NOTE

England's Bletchley Park was the centre of decoding and encryption for the Allies during World War II. The success of the Allies in ultimately winning the war was predicated on the work done there by amazing code breakers, agents and operatives. Five of the characters in my story are based on real people.

"Bertie" was King George VI.

Commander Edward Travis was an intelligence officer, a cryptographer and the head of Bletchley Park for the latter years of the war. His organizational skills were responsible for making Bletchley Park more effective in helping to win the war.

Alan, otherwise known as the Professor—the man on the bike wearing a gas mask and pyjamas, in charge of Hut 8—was Alan Turing, credited not only with playing a critical role in helping the Allies win the war, but also with being the father of modern computing. He was a true genius who saw things that others couldn't even conceive of. It is thought that his work helped bring the war to an end years earlier, and in doing so he saved hundreds of thousands, if not millions, of lives. His life, and the tragic turn of events that followed after the war, should be explored by those interested in learning more about this brilliant and unique individual. Numerous books have been written about him.

"Little Bill," Sir William Stephenson, has been an active character in all the Camp X novels. He was the real spymaster, born in Winnipeg, Manitoba, who is credited with being one of the single most important individuals in the Allies' war efforts, a great Canadian hero. Ian Fleming, along with hundreds of other spies and operatives, trained under him. The definitive work on Stephenson is *A Man Called Intrepid*, written by William Stevenson.

Finally, Ian Fleming is, of course, the creator of

literature's greatest fictional spy, James Bond, 007. In reality, Mr. Fleming was a master operative working for Naval Intelligence. It was Fleming who, in a 1939 memo, conceived of the famous strategy known as the "Man Who Never Was"—a strategy that involved using a dead man to plant false information, which gave me the inspiration for my story's ending. Fleming's contributions as a writer—and they are significant—are less monumental than his contributions to the winning of the war.

It was such a pleasure, and an honour, to include these real people in my story. I only wish I could have had the opportunity before he died to sit down with William Stephenson, share afternoon tea in the Princess Hotel in Hamilton, Bermuda, and ask him to perhaps share a story or two—promising never to tell those stories to anybody else.

These men were heroes of the highest order. They overcame an evil more profound than any that I could ever have conceived as a writer. Without them, it is probable that I would not have the freedom to write, nor you as a reader the freedom to read, learn and grow from their stories.

A message for my readers
from Eric Walters

I *love* writing. While I'm glad when teachers and other adults like my books, I'm even happier when children and young adults like them. Those are the people I write for. When I was a teacher I read each of my books to my students while I was writing them to find out what they liked, what they didn't like, what confused them, and to help me become a better writer. Now, writing full-time and out of the classroom, there's a danger of a gap growing between me and my readers. I want to close the gap. I really want to know what *you* think of this book.

What did you like, what didn't you like, what would have made the book better, and what do you think I should write about next? Email me at ericwalters@uniserve.com and let me know.

I promise that I will read your email and use that information to help me become better at writing books that you want to read. Your opinion doesn't just matter to me—it matters a lot.

Eric

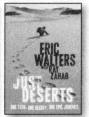